THE DARK AND DANGEROUS GIFTS OF DELORES MACKENZIE

Yvonne Banham

Firefly

First published in 2023
by Firefly Press
25 Gabalfa Road, Llandaff North, Cardiff, CF14 2JJ
www.fireflypress.co.uk

A CIP catalogue record of this book is available from the British Library.

1 3 5 7 9 8 6 4 2

ISBN 978-1-915444-07-3

This book has been published with the support of
the Books Council Wales.

Printed by CPI Group (UK) Ltd, Croydon, CR0 4YY

1

Delores always left her escape from the island until the last possible minute. She loved the race along the causeway, competing against the rapidly rising tide, daring the waves to push her off her feet as she dashed through the first slithers of incoming seawater.

This particular afternoon was sharp and blustery, with March winds sending storm clouds scudding along the Firth. Even by her usual standards Delores had left it late, huddled against the wall of the old lookout as she finished one more chapter. She stuffed the book in her pack as fat, cold drops of rain burst on the back of her neck. As she turned towards the causeway that linked Cramond Island to the mainland, she saw a dark smudge at the edge of her vision.

'Can't be,' she whispered.

The prickling on her arms told her different. A suggestion of a shadow, an echo of a person long dead, a Bòcan.

'What are you doing here?' she shouted. 'You never come out here!'

The Bòcan darted to the side, almost impossible to track in the storm-soaked light.

Delores swung her pack over her shoulders, pulled up her hood and ran down the steep bank onto the shale. The water was already lapping the causeway. She walked quickly, shoulders hunched, hands thrust deep in her pockets. Faster. Then running. There was a disturbance in the space behind her. Her hood was yanked back, and the neck of her coat was pulled tight around her throat. Something grabbed at her hair, dragging her back but she kept her balance – just.

Delores tried to scream but what little voice she had left was drowned by the cries of the sea birds that hovered on the updraft. Her hood slackened and a dark figure, more solid now, slid behind one of the stone pylons that lined the causeway. A man once, she thought, from its shape, its movements. She waited, watching for the Bòcan to show itself again.

Nothing.

Delores turned again towards the shore, towards

home. If she ran hard, she'd make it in a couple of minutes, but her feet were skittering along the stones that were slick with new seawater and the remnants of dead weed. She felt periwinkles crunching under her boots and the corvids that had been feeding on them rose in front of her, making nothing of the violent wind.

Delores sensed something reaching out for her as she raced towards the foreshore. Just a few more metres. She slipped as she hit the turn in the path and slammed down onto her right hip. There was no time to register the pain. Something tugged on her backpack and dragged her a few inches across the rough surface towards the water, scuffing her jeans and the skin beneath. The shock froze her for a moment.

'What are you doing?' she screamed into the wind. 'Let me go!'

Delores flung her weight forward and scrambled back to her feet. The sky had darkened to an inky midnight-blue and the row of white cottages ahead became vivid against it. She took a deep breath and powered up the slipway, her feet sliding back on the sand that was blowing across its hard surface, her legs shaking with effort. She reached the foreshore and raced towards home, the sound of her own boots barely disguising the footsteps gaining on her with every metre. She prayed that her sister would be home, that the door wouldn't be locked. The handle twisted and she fell in through the door. She reached back to catch it and slammed it shut behind her.

Delores slid down onto the cold stone floor.

'Could do with some help here!' she shouted.

Delilah rushed through from the kitchen and threw herself down next to Delores, adding her weight to the door as something pounded and rattled from the other side of the wood.

'Bòcan?' grunted Delilah, as the door banged the air out of her lungs.

Delores nodded. 'Chased me from the island.' The door thudded into their backs again.

'Thought you said they never go out there?' said Delilah, '"All that salt", you said. Wow, Delores, this one's strong!' A single violent bang on the door, then silence for a few moments.

Delores put her hand on the back of her neck. When she pulled it away, there was blood on her fingers. 'It grabbed me,' she whispered.

'Grabbed? Where?' Delilah leaned in to check for damage.

Delores swerved away from her sister and wiped her hand on the underside of her jeans. 'Probably just wanting to play. Like when I was little.'

4

'Play?' The door thudded into their backs again. 'This one feels pretty substantial,' said Delilah. 'Not like your old imaginary friends.'

'They were *never* imaginary... You had them too; I know you did.' Delores pressed her back into the door, already feeling the bruises in the knobbly bones of her spine.

'I did,' said Delilah, 'but I left mine behind when I grew up, and they never tried to hurt me. This is a bit different from your dolls' tea parties. You must be sending out some powerful signals to attract this strength of manifestation.' She took a breath. 'You know it's time, don't you? For you to go to the Uncles?'

Delores felt her stomach fold in on itself. The threat of the Uncles had been looming dark on the horizon for some time, ever since their parents disappeared. Delilah had dropped hints here and there, the odd mention, but she'd known better than to broach the subject full on. Delores knew what was coming. 'No way I'm going to those creeps,' she said. 'Forget it.'

Delilah shifted slightly, digging her heels firmly into the kitchen floor, bracing for the next impact. 'Those *creeps*,' she said, 'are the key to you having a tolerable life, stopping the worst of these things pushing through.'

'A *tolerable* life? Fabulous. What every girl dreams of.'

There was another single, powerful bang, smashing the door against their spines. Then silence. Delores and Delilah held their positions, their ears prickling, searching for signs that the Bòcan had gone.

There was a gentle tapping on the wood. Light and patient.

'Bit of a change of tactic,' whispered Delores. 'Should I take a look?'

Delilah shook her head and pressed her finger to her lips. They heard light footsteps walking away from the door. She frowned at Delores and whispered, 'Sounds like they're getting smart as well as angry. Tactical ghouls we can do without, thanks.'

Delores leaned forward to undo her laces, but her fingers were bright red and painful from the bitter wind.

'Let me,' said Delilah. 'You will have to go, Delores … to the Uncles, I mean. We all have to go through the process, like it or not.'

'Not. Not now. Not ever. I'm actually quite fond of who I am, thanks.' Delores tried to nudge her sister's hand out of the way, but Delilah held on to the laces, picking at a knot that was bound tightly by seawater and sand.

'It's not *who* you are that's the problem, it's *what* you are and *how* you manage it. Stop fidgeting and let me do it!' Delilah pulled her sister's foot onto her lap. 'Look how those things are changing. You're going to get hurt … and…'

'And what?' Delores searched her sister's face for clues, for a reason behind her hesitation.

'A letter came, from Norway,' whispered Delilah. 'I've been assigned.'

Assigned. That meant Delilah would leave, move on. It hit Delores like a rock in the centre of her chest. 'You didn't even tell me you were applying!' she said. 'How could you not tell me?'

Delilah tried to shift a long curl that hung over her face as she exhaled. She brushed the hair away in a gesture that was so like their mother it made Delores' heart ache.

'I didn't apply,' said Delilah. 'They contacted me after getting a recommendation from the Uncle I studied under in St Andrews. Barnabas always liked me. Thought I had potential.'

'You could say no,' said Delores.

Delilah stared at her sister's bootlaces, at the sand on the floor, anything to avoid looking Delores in the eye. 'I could if I wanted to. But I don't. It's the right time and it's a great placement. I'll learn so much, maybe even get as far as the Upper Council.'

Delores pulled her foot away. 'Upper Council?

You make it sound harmless. Call it what it is. The *Psychic Adjustment Council*. And that's exactly what they do, adjust people. It's what they'd do to me, given half a chance. If Mum was here…'

'Well, she isn't, and we don't know if they're ever coming back.' Delilah shifted up onto her knees so she could peep through the letterbox. 'We all have to go through it,' she said, 'learn to manage our signals, keep those things on the other side, where they belong. Looks like it's gone.' She flopped back down again.

'Could have told you that,' said Delores. 'The prickling's gone right along with it. It's given up.'

'For now, maybe, but what if it tries again? We don't know who they were before they died, what they did. The ones you played with when you were little, they were fine, probably died when they were children. These ones? I don't think so. That protection Mum put on the cottage won't last much longer; they're chipping away at it every time they come knocking.'

'If you mean the troll cross,' said Delores, 'it's still there. I checked. They can't get in. She made sure of it after that one bit me.'

Delilah put her hand on Delores' arm. 'Have you *really* checked? It's cracked. One of the loops is broken. And even if we could fix it, they'd still be waiting outside.'

Delores pulled her arm away. 'You're overreacting. It's fine.'

'It's not fine. The Council will only put up with so much. They have rules, guidelines, that need to be respected.'

Delores could barely stifle a groan. 'Seriously?' she said. 'What are they going to do to me tucked away here? Cramond's hardly the centre of the paranormal sphere.'

Delilah opened her mouth to say something, but the words didn't appear, just a light pink flush of her cheeks. 'Be careful,' she said. 'You'd be surprised what they can do. You have to sort this out whatever you think about the Council and you know it.'

Delores hugged her knees, peering out over the top of them at the comforting, familiar kitchen with its scrubbed oak table and ancient cooking range. Their mother's jars of potions and dried herbs still cluttered the shelves that their father had so lovingly made for her from driftwood. He'd collected tiny bird skulls, their bones as delicate as lace, just for Delores, and her mother had made space for them between the bundles of lavender and sage, never fazed by any connection the family felt with death. The dust it all gathered day by day slowly dampened any hope of their parents' safe return.

'What will we do with this place?' muttered Delores. 'It's all we have left of Mum and Dad. How will they know where to find us?'

Delilah tried to put her arm around her sister's shoulder, but Delores shrugged her off. 'We can't just sit here waiting and hoping they'll walk through the door one day. I need my own life. I love you but I can't look after you forever.'

'Who asked you to?' Delores got to her feet and grabbed her bag. 'When do I go?'

Delilah swallowed hard. 'Next week. It's at the Tolbooth Book Store in the Old Town. They were a bit reluctant at first, but they said they'd make space for you.'

'How very accommodating of them,' said Delores.

Delilah closed her eyes, sighing away the last few breaths of patience she had for the conversation. 'You know what that part of the city's like, Delores; no one'll even notice you. Tourists expect to feel strange things. They *want* to be creeped out.'

'I don't creep people out.'

'You sure? How many friends have you got? And the weekend job at the café didn't last five minutes. You blend in in the Old Town. You always have.'

As much as she'd like to disagree with anything her sister had to say right now, Delores knew it was true. She'd spent hours, days, wandering those streets, running her hands along the old walls, waiting for the tingle that told her something might be waiting on the other side. Areas like Edinburgh Old Town smudged the lines between Paranormals and Normals, both governments happy for them to exist alongside each other as long as certain proprieties were observed. A lot of ancient towns and cities had similar areas, York, Reykjavik, Tromsø. Delores did stay out of the graveyards, even though she was drawn to them. They made her anxious, as if she might be over-run somehow. The Bòcain had swirled around Delores for as long as she could remember: shadows, over-stayers from a past life clinging wraith-like to the present. It was her mother who'd named them. It was an old Gaelic word from her own childhood, meant to comfort Delores when she was too small to fully understand death.

Delores often caught movements out of the corner of her eye: someone slipping around a corner; a child waving, then gone; a magazine closing itself or a cup pushed to the edge of a table, teetering, teasing, spilling to the floor. Necromancy was its official name. That was her skill, communing with the dead, but a Bòcan was much more than a voice or a casual haunting. Simple ghosts were explained to her as echoes, stuck memories with no realisation of death. Bòcain knew they were dead, and they didn't like it. They were drawn to the living, to certain people. People like Delores Mackenzie.

Bòcain had kept Delores company when other children refused, when promises of *another time* never materialised. Delores accepted the strange creatures into the empty space where friendship should have sat, never questioned their presence or feared their arrival. But there'd been a shift. An elemental change. Was it when she was thirteen? When she turned fourteen? Delores couldn't quite put her finger on when it happened, but she knew the Bòcain wanted more than games and stories. She just didn't know what yet.

Delores put her hand to the back of her neck again and winced, prompting Delilah to force a hug on her whether she wanted it or not.

'Just look at you,' said Delilah. 'I can't keep you safe any more. The Uncles can. Maybe it'll just be for a few months, until you get things under control. Don't be mad, but I already applied to take you out of school. After the stuff that's been happening around you, and the nonsense from the other girls, they didn't put up much of a fight.'

It tugged at Delores that she was deemed so disposable. She pushed her sister away.

'Do I have a choice?' she asked.

Delilah shook her head. 'Not this time. It's arranged, all of it.'

Delores needed to snatch something from the jaws of her inevitable defeat.

'If I am going, the least you can do is promise me something.'

'Sure.' Delilah shrugged, eager to smooth the waters.

'Try to find out what happened to Mum and Dad. Someone must know. If they were dead, don't you think I'd have seen them by now?'

2

In the few days that followed, Delores took advantage of her sister's guilt over their impending departures. She got the haircut she wanted, bristle-short against the back of her head. So short, she could feel the outline of her skull.

'Occipital,' she whispered. She loved the sound of the word, the feel of the bone. Her finger slipped down to the scratch below her hairline, still raised from her encounter with the Bòcan on the causeway. She shook her head from side to side, dissolving the memory, enjoying the feeling of her thick dark curls falling forward from the crown of her head to her face. She ran her hand over the short sides and winced as her finger caught the new cuff piercing in her right ear. She was pleased with the overall effect and its added bonus of self-preservation, but Delores could hardly tell her classmates that it was to stop violent apparitions grabbing her by the hair. They'd been happy to add her new look to the long list of Things-That-Make-Delores-Mackenzie-a-Total-Loser. Until now, she'd managed to keep her paranormal signals bottled up until she got home, but something had shifted in the fibres that lined her veins and ran through her muscles. An essence that the other girls didn't have, the *normal* girls, the girls who didn't see the dead, or dream other people's dreams, or read the future. The girls who existed alongside the Paranormals, the psychics and the seers, without ever noticing them. They couldn't quite figure out what it was about Delores Mackenzie, but they sniffed out her difference like foxes hunted prey. Even technology was making moves against her, stalling whenever she came near. The school library system had crashed when her hand made the lightest of contact with the barcode reader as she tried to check out an edition of Edgar A. Poe's *Works*. The deliciously gothic, leather-bound volume had slipped seamlessly under her jacket amidst the chaos. It was her last day at her old school – and the best.

Sitting on her bed, possibly for the last time, Delores ran her hand over that same book. She'd found it in the

Benefactor's Corner of the library, a space dedicated to books from grand old houses around Edinburgh and their long-dead owners. It was a quiet space, unpopular, and she loved it. She hadn't been looking for anything specific that day and her hand had been drawn to the book before her eye was. As she'd opened it, she'd been beguiled by the aging pages' vanilla scent and the tingling in her fingertips as she touched the endpapers. There was a faded inscription on the yellowed title page: *To my darkest Angel, my Lady of the Tower,* and it thrilled her every time she saw it. Delores was glad she'd rescued such a book from the unappreciative hands of her ex-school and her ex-life, but as she held it her arms felt heavy, and a deep discomfort settled into the pit of her stomach. It wasn't guilt; what had she to feel guilty about? It had been an act of liberation. *Probably just nerves* she told herself. Meeting new people was pretty much at the top of her list of least favourite things. She slid the book into her rucksack, next to the envelope stuffed with cash. Delilah had given it to her for 'extras', with the promise of more to follow. Cash machines and payment gadgets threw up a whole other realm of problems, either cloaking themselves in frost or hissing out sparks as they spat Delores' mangled bankcard back at her.

Delilah tapped on the bedroom door to hurry her sister along. Delores wrapped one of her smallest, most fragile bird skulls in a silk scarf soaked in her mother's perfume and placed it with great tenderness into her coat pocket. She closed her eyes and focused on the sounds of the birds and the sea, the creaks and sighs of the cottage, banking each and every one as a precious memory.

Growing up, Delores had woken every morning to the smell of breakfast drifting up through her floorboards from the kitchen. She would huddle under her quilt, listening to her parents chatting about the day ahead as they prepared bacon or sausages to fill freshly warmed crusty bread rolls along with coffee too strong and too bitter for Delores' palate. But she'd drunk it anyway.

One morning, a little over a year ago, Delores overslept.

There were no noisy parents, just a missing suitcase and a few clothes abandoned on the floor. As the sisters scoured the cottage for clues, they found a scribbled note hidden under a placemat on the kitchen table. *Remember, we love you* was all it said.

Delilah had contacted the Department of Illusory and Treacherous Mislocations to try to find out what had happened to their parents but all they would say was that they could report no trace of them, living or dead. They decreed that, at seventeen, Delilah was quite old enough to be responsible for Delores and a small financial allowance was granted. Then followed a year of unanswered questions, gaping silence, and creeping doubt.

Delores slumped her way down the stairs and out of the cottage into the watery March sun. The wailing lament of the gulls overhead provided the perfect soundtrack as Delores felt the last threads anchoring her to her family disappear on the spring tide.

The journey into Edinburgh was painfully short. Delores sat in silence, head down, her feet on top of her shabby case in the back of the black cab. Delilah chatted on regardless with advice on what to say, what not to say, and about how she had no clue which Uncle was currently in residence in the Old Town. But she was sure that the Tolbooth Book Store would be fascinating, and great, and all the other platitudes she could think of.

Delilah had spent two years with an Uncle at another bookshop, in St Andrews. She'd loved it, but then her levels of psychic energy had not been as challenging as Delores'. All she would ever say about the Uncle that was assigned to her was that he was called Barnabas, he was unusual, and that she got used to him. She would never be coaxed on exactly what she meant by *unusual*. Delores knew that her sister still wrote to Barnabas, and received beautifully handwritten letters in reply, always stamped at the bottom with a picture of an otter.

Delilah concluded her ramblings with, 'Sorry but I can't come in with you.'

'What?' snapped Delores.

'*To be left alone at the door*. It's the rules.'

'Rules? Nice of you to let me in on them!'

Anything Delilah said after that was drowned out by the noise of the taxi rumbling over the cobbled street. Delores leaned against the door and watched as the tall, tightly packed buildings shuddered by, stretching upwards like vertebrae, with their ribs of narrow closes, wynds and courts encasing a delicious network of underground vaults and hidden passages. This dark underbelly of the city seethed with ghouls and over-stayers that eager tourists merely sensed but that Delores knew to be a constant presence. It gave her the feeling that the world was perpetually shifting beneath her feet.

As the taxi came to a halt, Delilah leaned over and hugged her.

'It'll be fine,' she said. 'Just do what they ask, and maybe you can join me in Norway.'

Delores pulled back from the hug.

'Like that's going to happen any time soon.'

She clambered out of the cab and slammed the door with bone-rattling ferocity, satisfied to see Delilah jump and then shuffle uncomfortably in her seat. But the cab still drove away, and Delores was still alone.

The Tolbooth's conical bell tower loomed over her, its turrets and suspended clock making a brave attempt to overcome the dull grey construction of the rest of the building. There was a pend under the tower leading to a courtyard and, next to that, the Tolbooth Tavern. A Bòcan formed briefly from the shadows – a thin, insubstantial one. It seemed unaware of Delores and she felt no threat from it as it stood peering through the Tavern window. A stone forestair lead to a black, wooden door on the second level of the tower, and Delores thought her destination might hold some interest after all. But when she got to the steps, there was chain across the bottom with a sign in old script that read *Service Only*. She would have no choice but to make her entrance through the main shop.

Delores dragged her case to the dark-oak shop door and bumped it over the step. The heavy door was propped open by a stone gargoyle with pointed ears and stubby horns. Its muscular arms were wrapped around its knees and its pug-like face glowered at Delores. She stared at it for a moment then looked quickly away as its brows furrowed more deeply and it leaned forward towards her ankles.

Delores stepped inside, shaking off the prickling sensation that sneaked up her spine and pushed the hairs out at the back of her neck. She looked over her shoulder to check for the Tavern Bòcan but there was no sign of it. *Not him then,* she thought.

She took another look at the gargoyle, but it was still now. Its head was forward, and its hands rested on its knees as if it was sleeping. *Get a grip*, Delores told herself.

The light from the street barely made it past the entrance, but Delores could make out a girl and a boy, similar in age to her, standing behind a counter. The shelves below it were packed to capacity with a rainbow of brightly coloured books, much the same as the bookcases that lined the walls, punctuated by small white handwritten notes. It could have been any bookshop on any street in any town and Delores' mood was not improved by an added tinge of disappointment.

The boy was more interesting. He was studying a set of cards spread out along the counter's slick, black surface. The cuffs of his crisp white shirt were folded neatly back, and a pair of metal-rimmed glasses were balanced precariously on top of his head. The girl was reading a small book which she held at face height, pinched between her fingers. She looked sideways at Delores and tutted.

'You can't bring that through here, idiot.' The girl nodded towards the bag. 'Use the service steps.'

Delores was about to protest when the boy came out from behind the counter, pulling his fingers through his fine, white-blond hair, tucking it neatly behind his ears. As he came closer, Delores noticed a strangeness about his eyes. They were so pale she couldn't decide if they were grey or lavender and the black limbal rings that surrounded his irises exaggerated the whites. He caught her staring and she looked away as he held out a slender hand. Delores didn't take it. The girl's cold reaction to her arrival had backfooted her and she wasn't about to let the boy do the same. He smiled and shoved the offending hand back in his jeans pocket. 'Don't mind Prudence,' he said. 'She's not good with strangers on the best of days, and this isn't – the best of days, I mean. Sorry, I'm Gabriel.'

Delores felt flustered on Gabriel's behalf and a little bad about the rejected handshake. She half-smiled back instead. 'I'm Delores,' she said. 'I think the Uncle is expecting me.'

Prudence sniggered. '*Delores*? What kind of name's that?'

Delores' face flushed. 'No worse than *Prudence*.'

One corner of Prudence's mouth turned up and she reached for a small brass bell on the counter. She lifted it, paused, and then shook it. No sound came out but there was movement in the shadows at the back of the store.

A dry voice with a faint accent that Delores couldn't quite place said, 'Thank you, Prudence dear. Send her through.'

Delores tried to see who was there, but the shadowy figure moved further back.

'He doesn't like to come to the front of the shop,' said Gabriel. 'Not in the daytime. People stare at him.'

'Not scared are you, *Delores*?' The sneer in Prudence's voice was unbearable.

'No, *Prudence*, I'm not.'

Prudence's smug smirk made it clear that Delores hadn't quite pulled off the confident air she was aiming for. She put her bag on the floor next to her case and marched through the shop to the back room, cringing with every step.

Prudence tutted again and went back to her book.

The second room was darker, and smelled of vanilla, gentle spices and fresh tobacco. The whole room was encased in bookshelves, the uppermost shelf curving marginally outwards, creeping into the vacant ceiling space. A wooden ladder had been left leaning against a section marked *Transformation, Transfiguration and Metamorphosis.* Next to the ladder was a glass case containing several highly ornate books embellished with metal filigree clasps and locks. All of the books in this room looked much older than the ones at the front of the store, and Delores' mood lifted at the sight of their thick spines in muted reds and yellowing browns. The titles of these seemingly less valuable tomes had long since faded into a scattering of golden dust that shimmered in the flickering candlelight. In the shadows, Delores could make out a table, and someone was sitting on a tall stool at the far side of it. The Uncle.

'Come closer, Delores Mackenzie,' the Uncle said. 'Then I can introduce myself.'

Delores stepped towards the desk and as the Uncle leaned forward, she could see his pale, smooth face, with no signs of the wrinkles that his thin voice had suggested. His head was bald, shiny and freckled. His mouth was tiny, his delicate nose upturned, and his lips were thin and pink. He wiped something from his cheek and put a monocle up to one of his black button eyes. Looking from her side of the monocle, Delores could see his eye was rimmed with red and she wondered if it'd been a tear that he'd wiped away.

Once Delores had been sufficiently appraised, the Uncle lowered his monocle and let it hang loose on its golden chain. He tucked a photograph inside the pages of the book he'd been reading and closed its heavy cover. He drew his hand slowly across it with an affection Delores had rarely seen for an inanimate object and she wondered if it was the book or the photograph that had prompted the tear.

'Oddvar Losnedahl,' he said, 'but you may call me Uncle Oddvar. So very pleased to meet you.' Oddvar stretched out his hand. His nails were long and narrow, painted in glossy black varnish, and his skin looked like dried leaves, pale green and dull. Delores shook his hand. His grip was surprisingly strong. Oddvar held on to her for just a second too long, searching to make the eye contact that Delores was avoiding. When he finally let go, he looked to the side of her. 'You are supposed to be alone, my dear.'

'I am,' said Delores. 'My sister dropped me at the door.'

'Oh, I thought I saw someone with you. Just a shadow perhaps.'

Delores felt the air move behind her and a small cold hand slip into hers. She pulled her own hand away, and whatever had been there slipped back into the ether.

Oddvar shuffled round and hopped from the stool. He was shorter than Delores and slightly hunched. His legs were bent forward as he walked, and he held his hands together as if he were praying. He wore a black tailcoat over a green waistcoat and a high-collared white shirt. His trousers were pinstriped and tight to his stick-thin legs and his black boots had glossy buttons up the side. As he walked past Delores, she caught the scent of fresh hay. He sighed.

'Perhaps I was mistaken. Gabriel, please come through and show Delores to her room. Dinner is at seven, my dear. I expect you to find your way to the table at five minutes to the hour.'

Gabriel led Delores past a room to her left. It had a heavy wooden door, firmly closed, and a brass plaque which announced it as the *Private Chambers of Oddvar Losnedahl*. They climbed an uneven staircase, Delores bumping her heavy bag over every white stone step. The stairs lead them into a large dining hall with a long oak table, all six of its chairs pulled tightly in. There was an extravagant open fire, flanked on either side by armchairs, one of which was heavily stuffed and covered in cushions and knitted blankets, snug and inviting. The other was made of dark-green buttoned leather with a formal high back. It struck Delores as exactly the kind of chair suited to someone like Oddvar. It was not difficult to imagine him perched upon it, straight as a board, reading from a much-treasured book. The room was again lined with bookcases, but these were grander in scale. They were made of dark wood and the front of each shelf was carved with leaves, shells and small creatures. The uprights were interspersed with the faces of cherubs and figures of winged angels and reached all the way to the double height ceiling. The shelves drew her eye to a suspended balcony above. Gabriel saw her looking at it.

'That used to be for musicians at ceremonies and presentations would you believe? Not in my time though, or Oddvar's as far as I can make out. Just storage of old books and artefacts now, but you can go up there to read if you like.'

Delores nodded and they moved past the doorway of a bright, pristine kitchen with windows that must have overlooked the street. Gabriel pointed out his own room next to the kitchen and then Prudence's – both behind heavy wooden doors. The doors each had a small window, covered by a black metal grill.

Delores stopped to run her hand over the cold metal. The familiar prickling sensation made her pull back.

'They look like prison cells,' she said.

'That's what this place used to be. It's had tonnes of uses,' said Gabriel. 'Wasn't a very good prison. Lots of escapes, but that was centuries ago. Don't worry, hangings were carried out further up the hill.'

'No ghosts then?' Delores half expected Gabriel to take this as a joke.

'None that I know of, but then again I don't deal with the dead, neither does Oddvar. You?'

Delores was a little taken aback by Gabriel's frankness. Outside her own family, death and the dead were subjects most people found uncomfortable, conversations to be swerved or side-lined.

'The dead do seem to like me,' she admitted, 'but then there's dead and there's *dead*.' Delores groaned inwardly as soon as the words were out. Being the resident 'freak' at her last school had proved pretty exhausting and she wanted Gabriel to like her.

'I just mean there's more to the dead than simple ghosts…' *Groan. Shut up, Delores.*

Gabriel stared at her, and Delores died a little more inside.

'Anyway…' he said, 'Oddvar gets rid of any he comes across.'

'You sure about that?' Delores thought of the small cold hand that had slid into hers.

'Pretty sure,' said Gabriel. 'It annoys the owner of the Tavern next door though. Reckons he gets all of the Canongate's *restless souls*, kept moaning about some ghostly kids scaring his customers, but that was before … sorry, bet you don't want to hear all that. Probably just a few creaky floorboards.'

'Probably,' said Delores, wishing a few simple hauntings were all she had to deal with.

Gabriel nodded towards a smaller room with another heavy wooden door in the corner. The room was half-lit and cosy. The books in this room were different from all of the others she'd seen so far. They had spines adorned with perfectly preserved gold lettering and some volumes were turned outwards on their shelf, revealing lavish covers decorated with stars, planets and mythical creatures. There was a low table in the centre which was scattered with papers, several pairs of glasses and a small brass telescope. A crystal dish was perched on top of the papers, overflowing with nuts, seeds and dried fruit. Next to the table was a leather footstool, and on top of that was a mass of dried hay that resembled a giant bird's nest.

Gabriel opened the door in the corner and waved

his arm in an exaggerated welcoming gesture. 'This way.'

Delores sagged as she surveyed a steep, stone, spiral staircase. Her arm, her wrist and her patience were severely tested by each juddering step she took, bumping her bag up towards the door at the top.

'It's the only room left,' said Gabriel, as he walked ahead of her, 'but it's quite big. It's for two people but it's just you in here now.'

'Hooray for the empty bed then,' muttered Delores.

Gabriel stopped. His arms dropped to his sides and he stood in silence without turning. 'What did you just say?' he whispered.

'Sorry,' said Delores. 'I just wasn't expecting to share.'

Gabriel turned to face her. His face looked grey in the dim light of the stairwell. Delores tried to read his expression, to figure out what she'd said wrong. To her relief, his face softened, but the friendly smile was absent.

'Sure. Never mind,' he said, but it was clear to Delores that he did mind. He minded a lot.

Delores' room was much bigger than her old one at home. It had a window that overlooked the main street, letting in plenty of light, as well as noise from traffic moving over the cobbles below. The floor was highly polished dark wood, and the lingering smell of beeswax suggested a recent deep cleaning. There was a scattering of multicoloured rugs, faded and worn, and two beds pushed up against the opposite wall under a second window. Propped up against the pillow on the farthest bed was strange array of tatty-haired dolls in handmade clothes. Random dolls freaked Delores out. She'd loved her own, but she got a sense of unease around ones that had passed through a lot of hands, like they carried something of their past life with them. And these dolls were looking straight at her. She glared at them. They narrowed their eyes and glared back. Delores watched the biggest of them, a pale and lanky thing, reach out to hold the hand of a baby doll next to it as she dropped her backpack onto the other bed. But it couldn't have. It was a toy. And the gargoyle at the door was a doorstop and the creepy Uncle was...

'You OK?'

Delores jumped at the sound of Gabriel's voice.

'You look like you're gonna pass out.'

'Uhmm ... no, I'm fine. The dolls ... can I put them in there?' Delores nodded to a door at the far side of the beds.

'Please don't touch them,' said Gabriel, his

expression unreadable once more. 'They're not doing you any harm, are they? Leave them how you found them. Please.'

'You didn't see th—'

'It's locked anyway,' said Gabriel. 'It's the clock tower and the clockmaker took the only key last time he was here. Just the mechanism up there and a load of old boxes.'

Delores was about to ask about the dolls' owner, but Gabriel whisked past her before she had the chance.

'See you at dinner,' he said, closing the door behind him.

Delores waited, watching to see if the dolls would move again. She'd rather have the feeling of being completely alone, the way she'd felt when her sister dumped her at the door, than the sneaking suspicion that she wasn't going to feel alone again for quite some time.

'Go on, I dare you,' she whispered, looking for the slightest movement, a flicker of an eye, maybe the rounding of a tiny rosebud mouth.

You're being ridiculous she told herself.

Even so, Delores knew she'd never sleep with the dolls watching her. She looked around the room for something to cover them with but couldn't find anything. She took the small bundle from her pocket and slowly unwrapped it, being careful not to break any of the delicate bones or the needle-fine beak it contained. She put the bird skull on the small table at the side of her newly claimed bed. Her hand trembled and the feeling of being watched refused to go away. She took the silk scarf and inhaled its scent before dropping it over the faces of the dolls. She thought she saw it billow slightly from a puff of air underneath, but it settled like a shroud over the gawping faces. She sent a prayer to whatever it was she didn't believe in, hoping that her mother's perfume would protect her somehow.

When Delores climbed onto her new bed, her knees sank into the pale pink embroidered quilt. It was silky and smelled of fabric conditioner with slightly musty undertones. Loose threads from the delicately stitched flowers and leaves hinted at decades of gentle use, their colours fading against their dusky background. It perfectly matched the wood-framed bed that looked at least a hundred years old. The springs creaked as she crawled to the window behind its head. It had the now-familiar black bars, but these ones were twisted into a candy cane shape. She pushed her nose between the bars to get a better look.

When she looked down, Delores realised exactly where she was. Her room was above Canongate Kirkyard. It was tricky to get a good view, so she pressed her face hard against the bars. She could see a scattering of old headstones. Shadows moved across the grass and over the backs of visitors who were bending down to check the inscriptions of the poor souls buried under their feet. Her eyes were drawn to a small figure by the far wall – a girl. It was hard to make out the girl's face, but Delores could see that she had long brown hair, hanging loose and a little dishevelled. She wore a yellow coat and jeans, and her shoes were hidden in the grass.

The girl looked up towards the high window, waved, and started running towards the building.

Delores blinked and the girl was gone.

QUEEN OF COINS

3

Delores decided to put the bird skull on her pillow before she went for dinner. Staking her claim over her side of the room gave her some comfort, warning those wretched dolls to stay on their own patch. They'd given no indication that they were going anywhere, but she still didn't trust them.

It was dark outside as Delores headed for the dining room. She ran her hand along the wall as she descended the spiral steps, a delicate touch, hoping to feel nothing, no psychic imprints on the fabric of the walls, no echoes of past lives to make her trip and fall. There was nothing remarkable, maybe a faint buzz but not enough to put her on her guard. Maybe Oddvar did keep a clean house after all.

The rooms and the white corridors below were

dimly lit with a mixture of tiny bulbs hanging bare from ceiling roses and strings of fairy lights against the walls. The warm glow made Delores feel a little more relaxed. It was comforting, how her mother might have decorated it.

Then the sensation, the feeling: not a warning as such, just the knowledge that she wasn't alone. A shadow was following at a discreet distance and Delores was sure it wasn't her own. The shadow didn't reach out to touch her or grab at her clothes like the Bòcan on the causeway, but she felt its presence – soft and gentle as an echo. A child, once.

Delores reached back, expecting to find the small cold hand that had held hers in the shop earlier. The shadow backed away. 'I don't know who you are,' whispered Delores, 'but it was you that held my hand in the shop earlier, wasn't it?' She turned, hoping to find some detail amongst the darker recesses of the corridor. There was a thickening of the greyness, like something was struggling against the obscurity of the dark, but nothing more. Delores kept her voice soft. 'The Uncle said I was supposed to be alone. I don't think he'd appreciate an extra guest at dinner.'

Delores felt warm air as light as a whisper on the back of her neck as the Bòcan settled momentarily on her shoulders. She felt comforted, less lonely, but then the shadow drifted away.

Delores looked behind her and saw an insubstantial figure, the suggestion of a child, tinged with yellow where its coat would be. She reached out to it, but the figure dissolved with a hollow sigh into the dark edges of the corridor. The sound stirred a deep sadness in Delores, a feeling she was expert at pushing away.

Delores was the last to join the diners. Oddvar sat at the head of the long oak table in a high-backed chair, his feet hovering several centimetres above the ground. Gabriel and Prudence were sitting side by side, facing Delores. Their heads were together, as if in conversation, but Delores heard nothing. She barely glanced at them. Her eyes were fixed on the opposite end of the table to Oddvar, to the seat occupied by a bird.

The bird was perched on three brightly embroidered cushions, carefully measured to bring it from chair to table height. It was bigger than any native bird Delores had ever seen, as big as a vulture, but black – and reading a book. Delores looked at the other diners, Oddvar, Gabriel, Prudence, but no one seemed in the slightest bit perturbed by the strange sight, or even interested.

Delores worked hard to register what was in front of her. She thought back to what Delilah had said about 'getting used to the Uncles' but surely this must be beyond anything Delilah had experienced. She guarded her reactions. She didn't want to look like a total rookie but, hard as she tried, she couldn't bring herself to look away.

The bird had the dense glossy feathers of a corvid, their sheen glowing purple-black in the firelight. The feathers around its thick throat and above its sturdy black beak were shaggy and they ruffled gently in the warm air from the open fire. The bird peered at its book through a magnifying glass that it moved slowly down the page with its claw.

'Rude to stare,' hissed Prudence.

Alerted to her arrival by Prudence's hissing, Gabriel looked up and smiled, apologetic but not enough on Delores' side to say anything against Prudence.

Oddvar coughed politely, placing his delicate hand over his mouth. The noise was perfectly gauged to catch everyone's attention. 'Let me introduce you,' said Oddvar, nodding towards the bird. 'Delores Mackenzie meet Solas Sigurdarson. You may call him Uncle Solas.'

Oddvar turned his attention to the bird. 'Delores

is our new student, Sol,' he said. 'She has issues with the creatures on the other side. They seem to crave her attention somewhat. They invite themselves across her psychic boundary.'

The bird turned his head and nodded. He stared at Delores, courteous but silent. Then he clicked his beak twice, a hollow percussive sound that made her jump. His throat feathers puffed out like an Elizabethan ruff then settled just as quickly as he gestured towards the chair next to him with his head. Delores accepted the invitation. She was wary of his arched, glossy beak, as exaggerated in size as the rest of him, but she was keen to avoid another lingering handshake from Oddvar. There was also the added intrigue of what a bird would choose to read.

The pages of Solas' book were covered with intricate star charts, marked out in gold ink against a sapphire background. The annotation was unfamiliar to Delores and she struggled to make any sense of it. As if sensing her prying eyes, Solas removed his claw and Prudence reached for the book and magnifier. He tilted his head against Prudence's arm, and she allowed herself a reluctant smile.

Prudence placed Solas' things on a side table next to the cosier of the two armchairs, then went to the kitchen. She returned moments later with a stack of white plates and placed each one with swift precision in front of the diners.

They sat in silence at the table. Delores could feel Prudence staring at her, but she kept her own eyes on Uncle Solas. Oddvar removed an elaborate pocket watch and tapped it with the nail of his index finger. He nodded and put the watch away. 'Prudence, if you please,' he said.

Prudence took the lid from a ceramic bowl in the middle of the table. The smell that escaped was a divine mixture of fruit, meat and Moroccan spices. Delores' stomach growled and her mouth watered as Prudence delivered the ladle's golden bounty to her dish, chinking the silver utensil against Delores' fine porcelain plate. Delores flinched in spite of herself. Prudence saw the tiny movement and the heat of her smugness radiated far enough to make Delores' cheeks redden.

Delores blinked as the steam cleared, expecting to see an exotic feast, but the food was turning grey, settling into a mound encased in a shimmering, quivering skin. As Delores leaned forward to make sense of what she was seeing, a blister formed on the skin. The blister expanded and contracted, and when her unbelieving nose was a breath away from it, the blister popped and let out a hiss of foul-smelling air. She flung herself against her chair back, looked around, and felt the mothy wings of panic rising at the lack of reaction amongst the others. Prudence continued to serve, deftly refilling the ladle and metering out exact portions, but never once taking her eyes off Delores, the pink tip of her tongue poking out from between her perfectly white teeth. She dropped the ladle back in the bowl and sat down. Delores shook her head.

'Something wrong?' asked Prudence.

'No, I … the food…' Her eyes darted around the table again. She pinched her own leg to make sure that she was awake, that the meal, Solas, everything since she'd left her room, wasn't a hallucination. The pain she felt in her leg assured her she wasn't dreaming. Real? That was another question.

Prudence raised her spoon to her chin. 'Eat up, *Delores*. It really is delicious. I made it myself: old family recipe.'

Solas made a gentle cronking noise and gestured with his head towards Delores' plate.

Delores picked up her spoon. Her hand was shaking. The lights dimmed and there was a buzzing inside her ears. The buzzing that comes before the black floaters arrive in your eyes, moments before you faint, where cold sweat wells up on the back of your neck. She breathed in through her nose but that only intensified the putrid smell.

Her food moved. Delores blinked hard. *It did not just move. It did not just move.*

It moved again.

The hole where the bubble had been opened wider and two tiny antennae wriggled their way through it. This time, Delores kept her eyes wide open and focused on the antennae as they twitched, curled, uncurled. A bead-like head popped through. A beetle. Then flailing cotton-thread legs and a metallic green body that glistened like a jewel in the low light. The beetle pulled itself up to the surface of the food, pausing as if to catch its breath. Delores risked looking away. She needed to see if the others were as horrified as she was, but they were all looking at their plates hungrily, placing napkins, picking up cutlery.

The beetle inched aside to make room for another, and another, as dozens of tiny beetles scurried across her plate. They ate everything in their path, carving tunnels and pathways amongst the foul sludge that only moments ago had looked so inviting. Delores tried to speak, but her mouth just opened and closed as she looked around the table, unable to move.

Delores was sure someone would intervene, say something, say anything, but they were all calmly tucking in, lifting silver spoons of steaming insects to their mouths. Uncle Solas pecked enthusiastically at the offering, which was less surprising. Gabriel wiped the corner of his mouth with his thumb as a slither of yellow yoke-like juice escaped the popping body of a slithering bug.

Delores felt Prudence staring at her, and saw that her mouth was set hard, lips pressed into thin blue-grey lines, the pink tip of her tongue still pointing out from between them. She was completely focused on Delores, her own foul spoon held below her chin. No blinking, just cold amber eyes. Delores dropped her spoon, and tried to push herself away from the table, but she was stuck.

Prudence glared, breathing heavily through her nose as Gabriel crunched and swallowed his grubs.

Delores looked in horror at Oddvar.

Oddvar banged his hand on the table. 'Prudence! Stop!'

Prudence jumped at the sound, then looked down and giggled. When Delores looked back at her plate, she saw a beautiful gleaming mound of lamb stew, dotted with raisins and apricots.

'I must apologise for young Prudence here,' said Oddvar. 'That was a most inhospitable display of her talents. Illusionists do somewhat have the tendency to show off. However, Delores, it is crucial that you learn to block out such signals. You will receive instruction at the appropriate time of course, but there will be no more intervention in such matters on your behalf. We have found through experience with Paranormal pupils that learning is thus accelerated.'

Solas cronked and nodded in agreement.

When Delores looked back at Prudence, the mean smile had returned. 'Sorry,' said Prudence. 'Enjoy your dinner.' Prudence blinked slowly, drawing attention to the fact that she hardly ever did.

Oddvar nodded. 'I am sure Delores accepts your apology.'

Delores was too busy imagining the food creeping around in her stomach to consider anything Prudence had to say as an apology, but she had no idea if the thought was her own or one Prudence had put there. She pushed her plate away and swore to herself that she'd be ready the next time Prudence came calling.

4

Delores refused dessert, though everyone's plate looked delicious, loaded with slabs of sticky toffee pudding, smothered in melting vanilla ice cream: the rich, creamy type with tiny seeds. Prudence had hummed and yummed the whole way through it while Delores kept her eyes firmly on Solas, watching as he used his claw to lift an embroidered handkerchief to his beak, wiping away the tantalisingly sticky sauce. Uncle Oddvar had refused her request to leave the table and the final seventeen minutes of dinner were excruciating.

Oddvar nodded. The chairs were pushed back, and Prudence carried the plates to the kitchen. Delores followed her with offers of help, but Prudence waved her away with a sneer.

'There's a rota, idiot,' Prudence pointed at a piece of paper on the wall, 'until Cook comes back.'

There was a carefully mapped-out programme, handwritten in violet ink. Delores searched for her name and found it lined up next to breakfast the following morning.

'6 a.m.? Seriously?' The words were out before she could stop them.

'Why? Are you special or something?' said Prudence. 'Too good for kitchen duties? I should be honoured you're even talking to me.'

'Maybe you should,' said Delores.

'Well, I hope you know how to light a fire, Cinders. That's what you do first. Light the fire in the dining hall. Oddvar will be down at 6:30. I wouldn't advise disappointing him.'

'Anything else I should know? As you're being so helpful?'

'I think I'll let you find out for yourself. Won't that be fun, *Delores*?' Prudence turned back to the sink.

Delores ran her finger down the paper, hoping to pick up some clues. She had no idea what to cook, what the Uncles had for breakfast, especially Solas. Doubtful as it was, she hoped the list would give up some secrets. Gabriel's name was at the top, but below that there was an evenly drawn line through a name she didn't recognise – Maud. She let her finger drift across the text and felt a familiar prickling in her fingertip.

'Who's Maud?' she asked.

Prudence stopped clattering the dishes around in the sink. Her hands stayed in the water, suds up to her elbows. The air in the kitchen thickened, and the same buzzing that Delores had felt in her ears at the dinner table quickened her heartbeat. She watched as a piece of Prudence's immaculate hair slipped forward across her face. Delores could see it quivering.

'No one,' whispered Prudence. 'Not any more.'

'She must be some...'

'Get out.'

'But...'

There was a rattling sound as the plates, standing silently in the rack a second ago, knocked against each other. Prudence clenched her arms to her side and white suds dripped to the floor. The air was agitated by pinpricks of sound and the rattling grew louder. The noise bounced off the stone walls and hard surfaces of the kitchen. Delores put her hands over her ears, but it made no difference. She watched, mesmerised, as a knife levitated from the corner of the rack, quivering as Prudence shook, her back still turned to Delores, her hands now tap, tap, tapping against her legs. Delores saw a shadow cross the wall at the edge of her vision. The plates smacked against each other and chips of white porcelain splintered onto the work-surface. The knife crept higher, and its tip scratched against the edge of the rack, desperate to break free.

'Prudence, what are you doing?' Delores whispered.

'No, no, no, no, no, no…' Prudence chanted. Her voice was monotone, whiney, pleading. 'No, no, no, no.' Faster and faster. The knife scraped and quivered a few centimetres higher.

'No, no, no, no,' Prudence whined, her hands tapping so fast against her thighs that their edges blurred. 'Get out!' she screamed.

Delores stood rigid, frozen. The plates smashed against each other and as the shattered pieces flew into the air, the knife rose above them and turned its tip towards Delores. There was a moment of calm, less than a second when everything seemed to be suspended in mid-air.

The noise crashed back in and the knife headed straight for Delores.

The small, cold hand from the book store grabbed hers and pulled her to one side. The knife flew past, grazing the side of her scalp, just above her right ear. It thudded into the wooden door frame behind her. Prudence went slack, as if all of the things that kept a person standing had been snatched right out of her. She slumped to the floor.

As Delores stood shaking, the small hand slipped away. She reached up to where she'd felt the knife graze her scalp, rubbing a trickle of thick, sticky blood between her fingertips. Whatever had just happened, it had been no illusion.

There was a gust of air and Delores ducked as Uncle Solas hovered into the kitchen. He landed next to Prudence and placed his beak on her shoulder. There was a tenderness, a kindness about his actions. He straightened his feathers and placed his head against Prudence's cheek, nudging her, calling gently to her. It was a rhythmic cawing that came from deep in his chest, soothing and soporific. Delores sank to her knees and listened, drawn in by the sound. Solas turned to look at Delores. He stared at her and nodded. She knew she should leave.

As Delores made her way back to her room, she felt something, someone, behind her. The small Bòcan from earlier. She knew by the familiar feeling: the prickling; the hairs on the back of her neck. She opened the door to the spiral stairs that led to her room, but before she went through she turned, slowly, hoping to see who the Bòcan was. There was some blurring in the shadows, a thickening of the darkness around a small form, but no detail, not yet.

'Thank you,' Delores whispered into the nothing. 'Thank you for saving me.'

An amber light bled through the window from the street and lit the stone steps as Delores entered the stairwell. She took each step slowly, pausing, listening. There was something in the stairwell with her, hovering, waiting, hesitant.

Delores didn't want to startle whatever, whoever, was there. She stood as still as she could on the stairs, trying to control her breathing. She steadied her voice. 'It's OK,' she said. 'I know you're a friend. And I could do with one of those right now.'

There was a gentle rush of warm air that moved over Delores like silk. It ruffled her hair and the graze from the knife stung just a little in the disturbance. There was no grabbing, no fear. This felt like the Bòcain that used to visit her for tea parties, that watched her as she played with her dolls, and looked on as she read her books. The ones that came before. Before the changes. Before the house needed protection. Before her mother kept them out.

Delores turned to look but the shape moved backwards again towards the door. 'Don't be scared, and I promise I won't be either,' she said. 'Can you show me who you are?'

Through the amber light, Delores could make

out a shape in the doorway. She tried to bring it into focus, reach out to it with her thoughts. The Bòcan shifted and a smudge of yellow brightened before fading again, the suggestion of a face slipping away each time Delores tried to pull it into focus. She turned her head so that she could place the figure at the edge of her vision and then she saw her. A child, younger than Delores and the others. Around nine, maybe ten? It was hard to tell. A yellow coat. No more detail. A distant metallic sound formed itself into a soft whisper. 'She's coming,' it said.

Before Delores could ask who, the little Bòcan vanished.

5

Delores had left the light on in her room. She peeped round the door to check if the dolls were still on the bed. They were and she kicked herself for being so ridiculous, but when she looked properly, she saw that something had changed. Their faces weren't covered by the scarf. The lanky doll was sitting up and the scarf was wrapped around her like a toga. Her tatty hair had been brushed and she glared at Delores from under her fringe. When Delores looked at her own bed, the bird skull was gone.

'What have you been up to, you little witch?' she whispered to the doll. 'That was mine.'

Prudence, thought Delores, *it must've been. How could I be so dumb?*

It was puzzling though. Prudence was the obvious

culprit, but Delores couldn't figure out when she could possibly have done it. She took a sweatshirt from her case, threw it over the dolls, and used it to bundle them up in her arms. She dashed to the door, not sure if the dolls were moving themselves or if it was just her own movement bumping them around. She feared the worst as she placed them outside her door. There was just a little too much adjustment beneath the sweatshirt, more like a jostling for position than a falling into place.

Delores shut the door and checked the wood that surrounded it, hoping for a latch of some description. No such luck. She shoved her case in front of it and got ready for bed, not that she expected to sleep.

The night was torture. The Tolbooth clock had struck every hour. Not a charming chime, or a clear peel or a clang, just a whirring and a click marking the slow passage of time. Delores' ears prickled as she lay in the dark, searching for sounds of tiny plastic feet shuffling around on the other side of the door. She fought sleep as much as she could but drifted and finally fell.

Delores was woken by the sound of early traffic on the cobbled street below and the first signs of dawn creeping around the heavy curtains. It took a few moments for her eyes to adjust to the grey light and, as she blinked sleep away, she checked the door. The case was pushed to one side. She took a moment to digest what she was seeing, to wonder if she could have moved it herself in the night, in her sleep maybe, but she doubted it. She lay there for a moment, building her courage, then slowly rolled to face the other bed.

The dolls were back. Her breath hung in the air … then dissipated in a sigh of relief. *Prudence,* she thought, *and people think* I'm *weird.* She shuddered, unsure what was creepier, the dolls or the thought of Prudence sneaking around while she slept.

The clock whirred and clicked. Delores counted six. She grabbed her clothes from the end of her bed, pulling and tugging at them in a desperate rush to get dressed, but everything felt damp, clinging more desperately to her skin the harder she tried. She resolved to sleep in them from now on, or at least keep them under the blankets next to her. She missed the cosiness of the cottage more than ever and the warmth that drifted up from the kitchen directly below her room. Delilah. Her parents.

She threw a thick jumper on over her usual oversized white shirt (courtesy of one of Edinburgh's many charity shops) and tweed trousers with braces, the cuffs stopping just above her ankles. Her sister had labelled her wardrobe *Victorian urchin chic,* not exactly what she was going for, but it had made her smile. She added an extra pair of socks before pulling on her boots. There was still a little water in the jug from the night before, so she scrunched some of it through her curls. Her hair at the back and sides was thankfully still bristle short. She rubbed what was left of the water over her face and dry-brushed her teeth. Her lack of curiosity about the bathroom arrangements had definitely come back to haunt her at this ungodly hour. The fresh application of eyeliner was ruined by her shaking hands, which in turn prompted the search for her fingerless gloves. She moved closer to the mirror on the dressing table to check that she'd rubbed away any remnants of sleep. As she looked at her grim reflection, she saw a flicker of movement behind her, and a piece of paper slid under the door that led to the clock tower. She stared at the paper for a moment, like it might move, or disappear, anything but just sit there. The clock mechanism whirred, no click. The quarter hour.

Delores jumped up and snatched the paper, holding it to the bedside lamp. The writing looked young, single letters in thick red pencil.

She's coming.

Help me.

M.

'M?' whispered Delores. 'Maud?' She went back to the clock-tower door and tried the handle, but it was locked. 'Is it you, Maud? Don't be scared, I see people like you all the time. You're safe with me.' Delores pressed her ear against the door. She thought she could hear gentle breathing, as if someone was leaning up against the other side. She pressed her eye against the keyhole, feeling the cold brass plate pressing into her face. There was a movement as something dropped out of sight.

'It was you in the shop, and on the stairs, wasn't it?' said Delores. 'I'll turn away if you want to come in. I'll stand on the other side of the room. Please, let me see you.' Delores pulled back, rested on her haunches with her arms wrapped around her knees. She waited for a reply, a sign, but all she heard was footsteps retreating up the stairs towards the clock room.

When Delores got to the kitchen, Gabriel was already there. She thought about telling him about the small Bòcan, but it all sounded so … dramatic. Even for a Paranormal.

'Thought you might like some help,' said Gabriel. 'The range is warm all the time, so you can start on breakfast. Porridge, berries, white toast with salted butter. Coffee for the Uncles, hot chocolate for the rest of us. Don't sit down until last when you're on serving duty.'

Delores saw Gabriel register the vague panic she was feeling. It was a shame he didn't realise it wasn't all about the breakfast.

'Don't worry,' he said. 'You'll get the hang of it all. Cook should be back tomorrow, but it's good to know how things work around here. I'll go do the fire.' The opportunity to tell Gabriel what was going on slipped out of the door along with him and Delores' *thanks* was left hanging in the air.

The kitchen showed no signs of Prudence's conjurings from the night before. It was pristine, except for one thing. A feather. Delores picked it up, assuming it would be one of Solas', but the colour was wrong. It was dark at the tip with lighter downy barbs towards the hollow shaft that would have attached it to a body. She slipped it into her pocket and set about making breakfast – a huge pan of porridge, milk for the chocolate and coffee from an Italian style percolator heated on the top of the range. Gabriel rushed back in a few minutes later with a breathless, 'Oddvar's here. I'll take his coffee. Never keep him waiting.' He flashed a quick smile before rushing out again. Delores hoped he didn't smile like that at everyone and then cringed at herself for being so … grim.

Between them they set the table, and at seven o'clock precisely a pale and bleary Prudence arrived. Her clothes were immaculate, her crisp white collar and her neat pinafore dress a stark contrast to the worry etched on her face. She glanced at Delores and away again, checking her wrists and tugging at her cuffs. Solas hovered in and took his place at the end of the table, settling into his pile of cushions, legs tucked neatly underneath him. He nodded a stately morning greeting to everyone in turn. When he got to Prudence, he once again rested his head on her arm. As he moved away, Delores saw the glimmer of a smile flicker across Prudence's face. Delores hung back, waiting until Oddvar was properly settled in his seat.

Oddvar put his monocle to his eye, checked the contents of the table and nodded his approval towards Delores. She then dished up the glorious globs of salty porridge and Gabriel added a spoon of honey to each, moving from person to person. When she got to Prudence, Delores clanged the ladle into the bowl, hoping for a response. Prudence yawned.

'What's up?' Delores asked. 'Tired from playing with dolls all night?'

'Dolls? What dolls?' Prudence tucked something

inside her cuff whilst oozing annoyance, then turned her attention back to Solas.

Oddvar coughed. 'Please continue with breakfast service, Delores my dear.'

Delores served the steaming hot chocolate, its sweetness curling through the air, and when all that could be heard was the scraping of knives on toast, she sat down to enjoy her own breakfast. She was shaking with hunger and the pangs pushed away all thoughts of the beetle-infested feast of the previous evening, along with her resolve to keep her guard up against Prudence.

Delores took her first mouthful, sliding the salty porridge from spoon to mouth. It felt like velvet on her tongue, but the delicious flavour shifted immediately to an earthy mix of beetroot and metal-tinged tap water. She looked over at Prudence and was met with a flinty glare. Oddvar's words from the night before whispered inside Delores' head: *Block out such signals.* A deepening sourness in her mouth swamped any reasoning she was capable of with anger. She tried to swallow but it wouldn't go past the back of her throat.

'I know it's you,' she said through gritted teeth. 'Get out of my head, loser.' A cough forced its way through as she spoke, and a minor spray of porridge escaped from the corner of her mouth onto the tablecloth.

'Napkin?' sniggered Prudence.

Delores shook her head and tried to swallow but the bitterness grew in depth and stirred a retching deep in her stomach. Sweat formed on her brow.

Prudence slid the tip of her tongue between her teeth and bit down on it. Delores felt dozens of minuscule explosions in her mouth, like popping candy but as bitter as the smell of old sweat. She gagged and spluttered, splattering food across the table.

There were gasps of horror from everyone except Prudence. Prudence calmly lifted her own spoon, raised her left eyebrow and slid some porridge into her own mouth.

Oddvar cleared his throat and dabbed at his lips with a napkin.

'That was quite an ambitious play after the exhaustions of last night, dearest Prudence. Well done.'

Delores was mortified. She felt her cheeks burning as a globule of porridge dropped from her chin.

'Well done? What do you mean, *well done?* Look what she did to me!' shrieked Delores.

Oddvar held up his hand, palm turned towards her.

'I did warn you,' he said, 'that you would have

to learn to block these things. If you do not, then I fear you will experience some degree of discomfort during your pupillage, not to mention starvation. As you are slender to begin with, I would give the matter your immediate and most undivided attention. I also recollect telling you that I would offer no further assistance with said skill, but as you have clearly made little effort, I suggest you think of it as hide and seek. Try thinking of shutting doors, closing curtains, pushing away the *uninvited*. You have the tools within your own mind to block such minor games. I suggest you master them swiftly. Toast?'

Delores raged deep inside at the injustice of the situation. She looked at the plate Oddvar offered. The sweet almost caramel smell of the thick white toast was divine. She took a piece and buttered it but when she lifted it to her lips, her mouth dried, and her stomach twisted into a hard, lumpy knot. The toast still looked beautifully plump, but her eyes and her appetite were no longer in sync. Knowing she would not be excused, she sat and waited for another excruciating mealtime to pass.

6

When the breakfast was cleared, Delores followed Gabriel to the front of the store, leaving Prudence at the back searching for some books from a list Uncle Solas had passed to her. Gabriel unlocked the door and lifted the small stone gargoyle from a basket filled with blankets, where it had spent the night. Delores thought she heard the gargoyle grumbling as it was lifted but put the noise down to the complaints coming from her own empty stomach. As Gabriel set the gargoyle down against the door, he turned it to face the morning sun. Its shoulders relaxed, and its head tilted forward, as it returned to its slumbers.

'So I didn't imagine it yesterday then,' said Delores. 'It *did* move. What is it?'

Gabriel rubbed the small stone figure between its shoulder blades. '*He* is a demon, from one of the minor ranks. Wouldn't say he's exactly harmless but...'

'Demon? You're messing with me.' Delores moved to get a closer look.

'I wouldn't get too close,' said Gabriel. 'He doesn't know you and he hates mornings.'

'Does he have a name?' asked Delores.

The gargoyle grumbled and turned his head. He stuck a long, pointed tongue out at Delores.

'Sorry about the tongue thing,' said Gabriel. 'Bartleby's not big on manners.'

Delores smiled and reached out towards the demon-gargoyle. Bartleby ground his teeth and she pulled her hand back. 'So how did he end up propping a door open in Edinburgh?'

'Oddvar did a swap with an old French academic from Notre Dame. A rare mystical text on angels in exchange for an actual demon. Oddvar likes that kind of thing. So here he is. Part of the family, eh, Barts?'

Gabriel scratched the gargoyle between the shoulders again and smiled as he wriggled in response. 'As an added bonus it turns out Bartleby's a bit of an expert in demonology himself. And he loves sherbet straws. He's open to bribes if you're stuck with your homework. Just don't play chess with him, no matter how hard he begs.'

Bartleby grumbled and pulled away.

'Oh, come on,' said Delores. 'I can kind of get my head round the rest, but chess? Really?'

'Why's *that* bit so hard to believe? Look.' Gabriel pushed Bartleby's basket to one side to reveal a checkerboard pattern painted onto the stone floor in black and cream. 'Bartleby's domain,' he said. 'Don't look so worried. You'll get used to us.'

Gabriel went behind the counter, took a cloth from underneath and dusted the levers and buttons of an antique cash register. The register was made of highly polished mahogany and Gabriel paid particular attention to some golden lettering on it that read *They See All*. When he was satisfied, he returned the duster to the shelf and opened a small safe next to it. He pulled out a brown cloth bag and pressed the 'no-sale' button on the register. A drawer at the bottom sprang open and he counted coins and notes into various sections in the drawer, snapping the notes into place with tricky-looking metal springs. There was a sign next to the register. *Cash Payments Only*.

'You only take cash?' asked Delores.

Gabriel stopped counting. 'We all have problems with tech. Bet you're the same. We've tried the new tills and card readers, but it only takes a lapse in concentration for it to go wrong. Oddvar got sick of getting them fixed. Make a note of what you sell on this pad and do the maths yourself. The numbers on the buttons are in old currency so it doesn't add up anyway, plus Oddvar reckons *Mental arithmetic is quite excellent for the brain.'*

Delores looked sceptical but had to laugh at Gabriel's spot-on rendition of Oddvar's dry, raspy voice.

'It's fine,' said Gabriel. 'People think it's *charming ... very Old Town*. Especially the tourists. We send them to the cashpoint over the road. They always come back and buy something. Especially if Prudence is serving them.'

'I can relate. She's very persuasive,' said Delores, 'and my own life's a bit *cash only*. Do we work in the shop? I mean, it's not a problem. I'd love it.'

'When we haven't got lessons. Or when we need to be *normal*, whatever that is. You'll fall out of love with it pretty quick.'

'Couldn't be worse than high school,' said Delores as she gazed along the shelves that encased the front room of the book store. The glorious multicoloured spines shone in the morning light, but Delores' attention was constantly drawn to the room at the back. The books in that room had promised fascination, age and darkness from the moment she saw them. It had only been

Oddvar's strangeness that had stopped her reaching up and running her hand along their spines when she'd arrived less than twenty-four hours ago. She stared through the doorway, tingling with envy as Prudence climbed down a ladder, moved it along its rail and climbed up again. Delores felt Gabriel close behind her.

'Just remember the books in the back are definitely not for sale,' he said. 'They're rare and highly specialised. Can't have Normals knowing what we get up to, can we? Make sure you get permission before you touch anything though. Solas is *really* protective over the hand-written stuff, and the translations.'

Delores was glad Gabriel had brought up the subject of the Bird-Uncle.

'Is Solas a *real* bird?' she asked. 'I mean, he's massive – too big for a raven or a crow.'

Gabriel hesitated and tried to make eye contact with Delores. She felt as if he was checking her out somehow, working out how much to say. She looked away.

'Mostly a bird,' he said, 'but he's an Uncle, just like Oddvar. Oddvar's in charge of everything but Solas helps with some of our lessons. Ancient astrological magic and maps mostly. It takes a while to get the hang of how he works and, just so you know, he'll only teach you when you're both ready.'

Delores edged her toe into the shadow of the back room, hoping to get another look at Solas. As soon as her toe crossed the boundary, Prudence whipped round to face her.

'Don't bother, *Delores*. Solas doesn't want you in here today. Says you're too disruptive. Too much of a distraction.'

Delores looked past her. Solas was wandering around the bottom of the ladder chittering while Prudence nodded.

Delores could barely contain her anger. '*Me* a distraction? You're the one planting visions and throwing knives.'

Solas turned towards Delores and raised his wings.

'Oh dear. It looks like he wants you to go,' sneered Prudence. 'And they're illusions not visions. Off you go, back to the nice shiny books and the tourists, Delores Mackenzie. I'm sure you can't cause any trouble there.'

Delores took a step forward, but Gabriel pulled her back.

'Don't. If Solas doesn't want you in the lesson, there's nothing you can do about it.' He guided Delores to the front of the counter.

'What is it with her anyway?' she asked. 'It's like she can't do anything wrong!'

'They're looking after her. She's having a really hard time.' Gabriel went back behind the counter and took out a pack of cards, slipping them from the box into his hand. They were bigger than ordinary playing cards, but Gabriel's pale, slender fingers stretched easily over their surface. Delores was transfixed by his elegant movements: how he tilted and split the pack. His nails were neatly manicured, and his skin looked soft, perfect. The cards were just as immaculate, no bent corners or thumb prints, but there was something about the colours on the back of the cards that screamed age, a background like clotted cream printed with a crimson red pattern. He shuffled them and placed then face down on the counter. He ran his hand across the top of the pack, spreading them evenly against the cold marble surface.

'Pick one,' he said.

'Tarot cards? Really? Bit hocus pocus, aren't they?'

'Maybe, but so are we. Hocus pocus I mean. Go on, pick one. Maybe I can guess what your specific skills are.' Gabriel smiled and tapped one of the cards.

'You think I'm falling for that?' asked Delores. 'I bet you chose that one just for me.' She looked at the cards and picked one several places along the line. Gabriel gestured for her to place it on the counter.

'Keep it face down though,' said Gabriel. 'More fun for me that way.'

'More like you've got them marked.' Delores smiled at Gabriel, but he shook his head.

'Nope!' He tapped the back of the card and stared at Delores.

Delores went to flip the card, but Gabriel placed his finger on the back of her hand as she touched it. His stare was fixed, and he spoke quickly.

'There are shadows following you, Delores Mackenzie: some good, some bad. There's a powerful female and she's looking for something. She wants to stay here, on this side. Family and friends are in the minus for you; you say you don't care but you do. A loved one is far away, looks a bit like you, probably sister. Death and change hover around you like smoke. You hate coriander, the word lobule and, cliché alert, you love gothic fiction.'

Delores felt her cheeks flush hot, and she knew red blotches would be splayed around her throat. She snatched her hand away.

'You knew that from the card?'

Gabriel smiled and shook his head. 'No. The cards are a hobby. I'm a seer. Never let a seer pin your hand down unless you want them to know *waaaay* too much about you. So – you've seen a bit of what

Prudence is capable of, and that's me out in the open, but I'm still not a hundred per cent clear about you yet.' He flipped the card over. 'Nice. Queen of Coins. Lots of good stuff with that card but, in worse news, mixed up with suspicion, doubt, and a hint of good old-fashioned terror.'

'Terror? Yeah right.' Delores picked the card up. It was silky smooth to the touch and printed in muted greens and gold. It showed a woman holding a jewel to her face and she was wearing a crown. Delores' fingertips tingled where she gripped the card. She handed it back to Gabriel and shrugged.

'Like I said, hocus pocus.'

Gabriel took the card and slid it back into the pack. 'Whatever. What *is* your thing then?'

'You were right about some stuff, but it's not smoke and shadows. I wish it was. Dead people like to hang out with me, and not all of them are nice.'

'Ghosts? Oddvar won't be happy.'

'Kind of,' said Delores, 'but a bit more *connected* than a straightforward ghost. They think and plan and do intentional stuff. Ghosts are just kind of stuck on repeat; won't bother you as long as you don't scare easy. Anyway, they used to come and play when I was little, mostly children – before they died. They were harmless, apart from one that used to scratch me, but I told him not to come any more and he disappeared. Problem is, now adult ones are getting interested in me and they won't be told what to do a lot of the time. That's what landed me here. I need to learn to *control my signals*. Stop them pushing through.' Delores tried to gauge Gabriel's reaction but he was still guarded: interested beyond politeness from what she could tell, but not shocked, which was a relief. *Freak no more*, she thought.

'So, what about you?' she asked. 'Prudence I can understand but you seem to have everything under control.'

Gabriel smiled but this time it was forced, none of the warmth Delores had seen before.

'My eyes,' he said.

Delores shrugged.

Gabriel pulled down one of his lower eyelids and leaned closer.

'I know you've noticed them. The colour, the dark bands?'

It was Gabriel's turn to blush. He pulled his glasses down from their usual resting place on the top of his head and tapped the frame. 'These are just a distraction for the customers, so they don't notice. Pretty useless when it comes to mystical afflictions. Truth is, the Uncles aren't helping me control my signals, they're teaching me to strengthen them.'

'Sure. If you say so. You can be just like Prudence. Great.' Delores ran her finger over the backs of the cards.

'Not great. All the seers in my family lose their sight sooner or later. Divinator's Curse they call it. I'm here to get ready. Stupid thing is the stronger my other signals get the quicker my sight fades. That's one of the reasons I like the cards, they're easier to see. I can read a lot of the books still, it's just fine print that gives me trouble. But who reads that, right?'

Delores wished she knew what to say. 'Not me,' was all she could manage.

'Pick another card?'

'I'd rather ask you something.'

'Ask away.'

'Who's Maud?'

Gabriel's face drained and he looked away. He pushed the cards back together, patted the sides so they formed a perfect stack and then placed them back in the box. 'You're right about the word *lobule* by the way. It's disgusting.' He shuddered and fake-gagged.

'Come on, Gabriel. Give me a break. I saw her name on the list of chores and when I asked Prudence, she totally lost it.'

Another pause. Another assessment of her trustworthiness.

72

'Fine,' he said. 'You're bound to find out eventually. Maud was a pupil here, kind of the baby of the family. She disappeared from the graveyard behind the Tolbooth. She told Prudence the day before that she'd been playing with some children from there but that they were scared their mother would come.' An intake of breath caught on the back of Gabriel's throat. 'Then she was gone. If we reach out to her, we can't find her. We don't know what happened to her, but we're pretty sure she's ... she's dead.'

Delores felt lightheaded, clammy. She perched herself on a stool behind the counter, next to Gabriel, and placed her hand on his arm. 'When? When did she go missing?'

'Nine days ago. She was here at breakfast, then went out to play. She never went far, and always promised to be back for lessons but...' He clenched his jaw and swallowed hard.

'I'm so sorry, Gabriel. I had no idea. What about the police?'

'*Police*? What would we tell them? That she was playing with ghosts and disappeared? She's a Paranormal; it's down to our own authorities and Oddvar seems reluctant to contact them. He never likes having them nosing around here, plus I don't think he wants to believe she's dead. He goes out every night looking for her. So does Solas.' Gabriel pushed the box of cards towards Delores. 'Turns out our skills are about as useful as these when it comes down to it. I thought I saw her going past the shop window the day after … her yellow coat, but when I ran outside to look, it wasn't her.'

'Yellow coat? Gabriel, I…'

Gabriel pulled his arm away just as Solas cronked from the back room. 'Uncle wants me. Can you open the shop?'

He walked away before Delores got the chance to say another word.

7

Delores found it hard to focus after her conversation with Gabriel. She managed to get the cuff of her shirt caught in the cash register twice and her fingers once. Her stomach rumbled so loudly while making each sale, that she attracted the sympathy of her customers. She refused one offer of a half-eaten sandwich and another of a dubious looking roll of toffees, fluffy from the owner's pocket. She distracted herself for the rest of the morning with a special edition of a Shirley Jackson novel that she'd found on reserve under the counter. Delores took care not to fully open the book and leave tell-tale signs of her illicit borrowing along the spine as she soaked up the story of the dark sisters hidden between the deckle-edged pages. It made her miss her own sister and she tried to unpick the tangle of sadness and fury created by Delilah's decision to abandon her. She pressed the book to her forehead and closed her eyes, desperate to push the feelings back down. She tried controlling them with her breathing: four counts in, hold for four, four counts out, hold again.

Her concentration was broken by the sound of scraping against the stone floor, and when she moved the book she saw Bartleby shuffling along the base of the door. He was grumbling, looking back over his shoulder, then edging along a little more, dragging himself at first, his claw-like nails scratching against the hard surface. He looked back towards the door again. Delores' fury was replaced by a sense of dread, a sense of something dark moving towards her. A shadow flickered across one of the shop windows and Bartleby scurried towards his basket. In Bartleby's absence, the door groaned ready to swing shut, but not before Delores glimpsed the edges of a Bòcan. It was mainly grey, its body still swirling but, as Delores watched, details started to form. A long coat, no detail, skimming the top of a pair of black boots that looked like they had red blotches on them. Blood? No. Flowers. They were decorated with flowers. Delores was trying to bring the rest of the figure into focus when the door slammed shut.

Bartleby pulled his baby-blue blanket over his

head and Delores heard him whispering and then chanting. She couldn't make it out, could have been French or something older, maybe Latin. Definitely not English and punctuated with small sobs. The hairs on the back of Delores' neck prickled and a small cold hand grabbed her arm. Another Bòcan, but this one had none of the menace or darkness of the one outside the door. It felt gentle, young, scared. Delores placed the book on the counter.

'Is that you, Maud?' she whispered. Delores felt a small body lean in against her and she could hear soft, gentle breaths drifting through the air which had become thin and cold. Delores kept her gaze down and glanced to the side. She could make out the sleeve of a yellow coat, the same yellow that had drifted in and out of focus on the stairwell. A pale hand gripped her arm. It was blue-white with cold and the remnants of glitter varnish, pink and silver, decorated its tiny nails. It was solid, not a shadow, a Bòcan but maybe more than that. Delores felt a head lean against her shoulder and long wisps of brown hair fell across her arm. Then quiet, almost inaudible, a voice. Delores had to bring all of her thoughts into focus, direct them at that single point of sound. The sound expanded and retracted, struggling to get through, one moment high-pitched, the next, moving away again. Delores let her head fall forward, blocking out the day-to-day background noises of the pavement, the tourists and the traffic. She finally pinpointed the words.

Don't let her in.

Something crashed onto the countertop and the moment with Maud splintered into the air. The hand was gone, and Delores was left with the deep sense of sadness she'd felt in the stairwell.

'What's up?' asked Gabriel. The pile of books he'd been carrying was scattered across the counter. 'You look weird. By that, I mean more weird than normal.' He grinned and started to gather the books back together.

'Thanks. I think Maud was here,' blurted Delores.

Gabriel stared at her. 'Not possible.'

'Possible? You're questioning me on *possible* after the whole Bartleby conversation? I've seen her a couple of times. I tried to tell you earlier, but Solas called you through to the back before I got the chance.'

Gabriel looked like he wanted to believe her, but then changed his mind. 'Can't be Maud. Why would she choose you? Why not Prudence? Or the Uncles? Or me?' Gabriel's voice trailed off to a whisper. 'We all loved her. You're a stranger.'

And there it was. Still an outsider. It hurt more than it should have.

'I don't know why,' said Delores. 'I never ask any of them to come. Maybe she doesn't want to upset any of you. Look at the state of Prudence when all I did was say Maud's name. Plus, not everyone can see them, just like I can't get inside people's heads.'

'Thought ghosts needed a reason to haunt you.'

'Not ghosts. I told you. A Bòcan *wants* something from the living, and some manage to force their way back.'

'Bòcan?'

'Goblin-spirit,' mumbled Bartleby.

'Maybe not quite a goblin,' said Delores, 'but I know what you mean. More like over-stayers, reluctant-dead. Bòcan's the word my mum used. It's Gaelic. The old language, you know?'

Gabriel nodded and re-stacked the spilled books in silence whilst Delores gave him the space that she knew he needed to take it all in.

'You sure it's her?' he asked. Delores could see his hands trembling despite his attempts to appear calm.

'Who else could it be? If she's here, she wants something. Let's just try and find out what it is. Please don't be angry.'

'I'm not angry,' whispered Gabriel. 'I miss her.' Gabriel's delicate hands hovered over the books then he nudged them all into line with one exact movement. 'Don't tell the Uncles. Not yet. Oddvar's super-cautious about attracting the attention of the Adjustment Council. Doesn't want then anywhere near here. If he thinks you're crossing a line with this, he might...'

'Might what?'

There was a fluttering in the doorway and Uncle Solas cronked a loud call. Gabriel put his finger to his lips.

'Lunchtime,' he said. 'Prudence is making sandwiches.'

Delores grimaced. 'I'll give that box of delights a miss, thanks.'

'Let's hope Cook comes back before you starve then. You might want to get working on that blocking technique.'

'I'll be fine,' said Delores. 'I might go for a walk. Clear my head and get some food away from Prudence's thrills and spills.'

Gabriel smiled. 'I'll try to speak to her, get her to back off a bit, but she can be tricky. Looks like Bartleby's decided we're closed for lunch anyway.'

'It's not that,' said Delores. 'Someone came to the door and he shut them out. That's when Maud showed up. She's scared of something, she's...'

Gabriel shook his head and pointed towards the

back room. 'Solas is just there,' he whispered, 'in the shadows. I can hear him breathing, his feathers...'

'His feathers? That's some hearing. Speaking of feathers...' Delores pulled the feather from her pocket. 'Is there another Uncle here that I don't know about?'

Gabriel snatched the feather away. 'No. No more Uncles. Talk later.'

Directly opposite the Tolbooth Book Store was a sweet shop called *Esme's*. Its windows were filled with trays of what claimed to be the best artisanal fudge in Edinburgh. It seemed to Delores that every other shop along the Canongate and all the way up the Royal Mile as far as the castle sold the 'best fudge in Edinburgh', to the point where she was surprised that the Tolbooth didn't.

She put her cynicism to one side and decided it would be the perfect place to get a sugar rush and calm her hunger shakes. A brass bell above the door rang as she walked in and she was hit by a wall of sweetness, not sickly but warm and oozing with caramel, rum, cocoa and butterscotch. The glass cabinets that formed the counter were filled with fudge cut into neat cubes, from the palest of honey colours to the deepest chocolate, infused with all manner of fruits, nuts and unidentifiable extra shots of sweetness. Rows of shelves on the back wall of the shop were packed tight with tall jars of old-fashioned sweets, from rhubarb and custards to pear drops, from sour apples to raspberry bonbons. As Delores ordered a mixed bag of fudge for herself, she spotted a jar filled with sherbet straws.

'Can I have six of those as well,' she asked the woman behind the counter. The woman's face was unremarkable, but her golden hair was folded into luscious thick rolls and her bright red lipstick gave her the look of someone who'd stepped out of a poster from the 1940s. She brushed her hands over her cotton apron and looked closely at Delores.

'Are you one of the Tolbooth kids?' she asked.

Delores thought for a moment and then shrugged. 'Suppose so.'

'Well then, you'll need the *blue* sherbet straws. It's what they all buy. Lord knows why. Hideous if you ask me.'

'I didn't, but OK.'

The woman was not disheartened by Delores' reluctance. 'Cash or card?' she asked. 'Or is that a stupid question?'

Delores said nothing, worried she might incriminate herself somehow. On a superficial level, it was a simple question, but it still made her worry in case it encouraged further curiosity.

As the woman passed the bag over to Delores, she held on to it for a moment. 'I'm Esme by the way. Nice to meet you.'

Delores took the bag and paid.

Esme leaned on the counter. 'So, if you're from the Tolbooth, you must know Sol.'

Delores shook her head.

Esme winked. 'Yeah, sure. Told you to tell me that, did he?'

'No, I have no idea who you're talking about,' said Delores.

'Sol! Dark, broody type. Tall though. My goodness isn't that man tall? Oh, what's his full name … something weird.' Esme drummed her fingers on the glass countertop. 'That's it: *Solas*. Solas, Solas Sigur – something or other. Definitely not local.'

Delores felt like her eyebrows had jumped up into her hairline. 'I think you must be mixing him up with someone else. Definitely no one like that at the Tolbooth.' She felt the need to examine the rows of fudge more closely.

'Mmmm. Whatever you say,' said Esme, winking. 'He can't avoid me forever! Enjoy your sweets.'

Delores made a rapid retreat and let the door

slam behind her. She shuddered and shrugged off all thoughts of Solas being anything other than a bird, even if he was an enormous, unfriendly, anti-social one. She put a square of fudge in her mouth, then another. Her jaws ached and her body sighed with relief as she headed towards the National Gallery.

Delores had been to the gallery enough times in the past with her mother to know she could get a decent hot chocolate and visit a couple of her favourite paintings while she was there. She'd also get some respite from Prudence and the questions, so many questions, that the bizarre conversation with Sweet-Shop-Esme had thrown up.

In spite of the time of year the streets were busy, and Delores wove herself in and out of the constant stream of people. She nimbly dodged pull-along cases, slow-moving groups and the random selfie-takers who stepped backwards into the road to make sure the facades of the Old Town made the perfect backdrop to their holiday shots. It always surprised Delores how people felt immortal when they were on holiday, as if normal rules didn't apply.

The pavements were slick with spring rain and the sun was failing in its efforts to remove the icy edge from the wind that seemed to be blowing straight in from Scandinavia. As she pulled her scarf around her, she imagined Delilah doing the same on the streets of Tromsø, sharing the far side of the same spring air. She headed towards the Playfair Steps, the quickest route to the gallery and a way that would avoid the crowds of tourists.

The cafe was annoyingly full, so Delores headed straight into the gallery.

The centuries-old paintings that adorned the walls of the first room – images of mothers and babies in golden frames, pressed together forever behind glass – clawed at the raw spot left by her own mother's absence. She let her grief swim free in the pit of her stomach for a few moments but when she couldn't stand it any longer, she headed for the steps to her favourite part of the gallery: Room 18.

Delores smiled at the attendant sat in the doorway and he waved her in. Directly in front of her was what she believed to be the most glorious painting ever, two angels dressed in dazzlingly bright costumes carrying a sleeping figure across the sea. It was everything she wanted for herself, to be magically lifted away, away to her parents, wherever they were. She tried to focus on the faces she loved so much, but something was drawing her eye away, disturbing her enjoyment. A sense of unease squirmed in her chest and a deep discomfort gnawed at her bones as she felt compelled to look at the next painting – a dark portrayal of a family where the painting of a fairy king and queen usually hung. She stepped back to get a clearer view.

The painting showed a woman and her three children in front of an old house with a tower. The children were facing outwards, all of them dressed in white gowns. Two girls and a boy. Their faces were pale, their eyes closed, and they held their hands outwards. The girls had long blonde hair that drifted around their shoulders and away from their bodies, as if they were underwater. Their feet were bare, and they seemed to hover just a few inches above the daisy-rich grass. The woman was standing with her back to the viewer, her dark chestnut hair woven into a low bun with tendrils curling around her back and shoulders. Her tailored coat was pinched in by two large black buttons where it met her lower back and was richly embroidered with tropical birds, their vivid feathers trailing down towards the hem. The hem drifted above a pair of black leather boots. The woman's right foot was turned slightly outward, exposing vivid red and green stitching on the boot, poppies in various forms with their stems twisting around the back of the heels.

'It can't be,' whispered Delores. She felt the hairs creeping up on the back of her neck and a shadow slid across the painting. The temperature in the room plummeted and the couple who'd been studying a portrait of Bailie Duncan McWheeble pulled their coats tightly around them and left.

Delores spun round and looked for the attendant at the door, but his chair was empty. As she turned back, she felt as if a hand were gripping her left shoulder, sending a dense, marrow-deep ache down her arm. Her breath came quick and light, forming thin wisps of vapour as she shivered in the freezing air. She was desperate to see what was next to her, whose hand was digging their fingers into the soft space above her collarbone, but at the same time too afraid to look up. Her arms dangled beside her, and she could feel her hands shaking. She looked at the floor, daring to catch a glimpse of this Bòcan, hoping it was insubstantial, a passing opportunistic ghoul that had latched on to her bad mood. What she saw was more terrifying than any ghoul. It was the boots. The boots from the front of the Book Store. The boots from the painting – grazed by the hem of the long coat, edged with a lacework of silver cobwebs. When Delores looked up again, the woman's head in the painting was slightly turned, glancing over her shoulder, looking straight at Delores. The hand on her shoulder dug deeper and a metallic voice whispered in her ear, *She is mine.*

Delores felt the deep, dull pain spread through her chest as her own ribs pressed in on her, squashing her lungs flat. She tried to turn her head to see what was holding her, but her body was rigid. The room darkened as Delores gasped for air. She tried to drag a breath in, but her chest refused to move and, just as she thought she would suffocate, the hand let go. She fell gasping to the floor.

The room warmed in an instant and, as if out of nowhere, the attendant was helping Delores up from the carpet.

'You OK, hen? What happened?' he said, looking panicked.

Delores looked around her. It was just the two of them.

'I tripped,' she said. 'I'm fine, honest. That painting … it's not normally there, is it?'

The attendant helped Delores to her feet. 'No. Well spotted! Been brought out of storage while *The Fairy King and Queen* gets repaired. Shocking what happened to it and no one saw a thing. Hard to believe, isn't it?'

Delores looked up at the security camera blinking away in a high corner of the room. She thought about the computers, the cash registers, the mobile phones, all highly vulnerable to paranormal activity. 'Not really,' she whispered.

'Sliced right through the middle it was. The conservators are beside themselves trying to repair it. We've had a few faintings in front of this one though. You know how it goes, a rumour starts about a haunting, and the next thing you know people are dropping left, right and centre.' The attendant gave a chuckle. 'Still, gets the visitors in, and postcard sales are off the scale.'

'Do you know anything about the painting?' asked Delores.

The attendant looked a little offended. 'Of course. It was painted in oils around…'

'Oh no, sorry. Just the story behind it.'

The attendant breathed out a short huff of irritation at Delores' interruption, but he regathered his smile and continued. 'That's Lady Barguest and her children. She was accused by her husband of poisoning them one by one, poor lambs.'

'Why would she do that?'

The attendant shrugged. 'Pure spite. Husband refused to divorce her. She was sentenced to hang for it, mind, locked up in Calton Jail. Escaped though, some fanciful story about a giant raven that used to visit her in her cell. No one could ever figure out how it got in there. Anyhow, they found her Ladyship's body in the vaults under the Old Town. Fair mouldered it was by then. Legend has it the body was encased in cobwebs, spiders claiming their own or some such.' He shuddered. 'Finally buried her in Greyfriars Kirkyard, unmarked grave, unconsecrated ground, but rumour is she still haunts the vaults.'

'A raven,' whispered Delores. She felt a deep-seated desperation for fresh air and the look on the attendant's face told her she looked like she might faint again.

'Don't fret, hen,' he said. 'It's just an old-wives' tale, a good one for the tourists. Can I call someone for you? You look a wee bit…'

'No, honestly, I'm fine.'

Delores made for the stairs then onwards towards the fresh air, casting a glance at the display of postcards at the booth on her way past. She didn't stop to buy one.

8

When Delores got back to the Tolbooth, she was still shaking. Bartleby was back at the door and Delores placed the sherbet straws at his feet. He put his hands on his knees and leaned forward to sniff the straws. He grunted and picked them up.

'Merci,' he grumbled. Delores thought she saw the glimmer of a smile.

Gabriel was at the counter like nothing had happened. He had his cards spread out again and was holding his hand over them, eyes closed. His disinterest in her return was only slightly less hurtful than the idea that he'd hardly missed her.

'Good job I'm not a shoplifter,' she said.

'I heard you coming. Don't you listen to anything I tell you?' Gabriel had a big smile on his face, but when he opened his eyes and saw Delores was shaking, his smile drifted away. He folded his arms on the counter and leaned closer to her. 'You look like death, Delores Mackenzie, if you don't mind me saying.'

'Very funny, and I do mind. You would too if you saw death as much as I do. Trust me, it's not always pretty.' Delores' head ached and she was so exhausted she could hardly hold herself upright. 'I think I need to lie down.'

'No chance of that. Oddvar wants you. He's in the back. Told me to send you through as soon as you came in.'

Delores groaned. 'I don't think I can. Not Oddvar. Not now.'

'Seriously though,' whispered Gabriel. 'What happened? That was some lunch break. You've been gone for hours.'

'Hours? No way have I been gone *hours*.'

'Whatever.' He turned his head towards the back room. 'Oddvar knows you're here. He just said your name.'

'I didn't hear him.' Delores staggered towards the stool at the back of the counter, but Gabriel blocked her way.

'He knows you're back. You'd better go through.'

Oddvar was behind his desk, exactly how he'd been

when Delores arrived the day before. Across from him, on the table, was a bowl of steaming broth and a plate of bread. Delores could smell the sweetness of every slice, each piece topped with thick slabs of saffron-yellow butter.

'The food is for you, my dear.'

Delores hesitated. She looked around the room, expecting Prudence to be hiding in the shadows, ready to catch her out.

Oddvar gestured for her to sit down. 'You are quite safe from Prudence. She's sleeping. I would not normally allow food outwith the dining room, or indeed proper mealtimes, but I thought we could take this opportunity to get to know each other a little. I fancy we have stepped off on the wrong foot.'

Delores' jaws ached with anticipation as the savoury smell of the broth hit her in waves. She picked up her spoon and gazed at the feast in front of her. Shredded beef rested amongst pearls of barley and fine slithers of carrot. Her hand trembled. She was conscious of Oddvar's constant gaze, of her own reflection in his monocle. Delores died a little inside as he closed his precious book and moved it to a small side table.

'I don't normally spit food out,' she said. 'You don't need to protect your things from me.'

Oddvar smiled and said, 'Quite so, my dear.' But he left the book in its new resting place.

The moment Delores took the first spoonful she forgot that Oddvar was watching. The salty creaminess of the butter, the sweetness of the bread, and the deep savoury flavour of the broth were all she could think about. She was wiping the bowl with her final piece of bread by the time Oddvar offered her a napkin.

'Thanks,' she muttered.

Delores knew she should be more gracious, but her strong sense of injustice kept dragging her back to the previous mealtimes.

'Why do you and Solas let Prudence get away with it? With being such a bully?' she asked. 'I know she's upset about Maud but—'

Oddvar raised his hand. 'Firstly, you will refer to your tutor as *Uncle* Solas. Secondly, I do not wish to discuss Maud or Prudence with you at this point in time. I am happy to discuss how *you* deal with Prudence. How *I* deal with her is not open to pupil discourse or indeed opinion. You may now ask me a question.'

'OK. How do *I* deal with Prudence then?'

Oddvar nodded his approval at the new question. 'Prudence has strong abilities. She can make you believe most anything she would like you to believe.

Taking this into account, I would say she has let you off lightly thus far.'

Delores pushed her empty bowl away. 'You have got to be kidding me,' she muttered.

'Please enunciate whilst we converse,' said Oddvar. 'And I am not in the habit of *kidding*, as you put it. Prudence can summon images that would strike fear into the heart of the bravest individuals, things that Hell itself would pale at. She is currently toying with you. The energy she uses is similar to your own; the signals are similar in nature and strength. She is a classic illusionist, with several other peripheral skills, some yet to reveal themselves I suspect. Gabriel can see inside people's minds, their very souls: his powers are divinatory. Your signals fall into the realms of necromancy, but we both know your skills go beyond merely speaking with the departed. You draw the dead to the living, make them feel alive again. Yours, in my estimation, is the most dangerous of gifts.'

Delores shook her head. 'I'd say knife-throwing temper tantrums trump necromancy.'

'That would be the obvious conclusion, if all you did was *commune* with the dead. Communing is within the scope of many Paranormals and would be a great deal easier to control: a simple dialling up and dialling down of your abilities, a matter of invitation over intrusion. But we digress. This is not a debate on the weight of our gifts, yet I will offer you this: Prudence can indeed be dangerous, but she is one person. You attract multiple dangers, Delores Mackenzie. Is that not so?'

The images from the gallery flashed through Delores' mind. She had the chance to tell Oddvar about the woman in the painting, how she had been at the door of the Tolbooth, but it seemed he already thought Delores was a problem, a hazard. He might send her away before she could help Maud, just like her own sister had sent her away when her signals had become problematic. The safest answer she could come up with was 'Maybe'.

Oddvar nodded, stacked the empty plates and moved them to one side. 'Then we shall begin our first lesson.'

Oddvar took a plain wooden box from one of the bookshelves and placed it between them. 'If you are to defeat intrusions such as those so expertly manifested by dear Prudence, you need to be able to deflect them. Push them away. Close your eyes, please.'

Delores was tired of hearing about the excellent skills of *dear* Prudence, but for now she would follow instructions and try to get on Oddvar's good side, assuming he had one.

'What do you see?' asked Oddvar.

'Nothing. Just black. Oh, wait, a silver spot.'

'Watch the spot, my dear.'

Delores watched as the spot grew. Within a few seconds, it was a silver ball, rotating in the air, in the dark space of her mind's eye. It stopped spinning and rolled towards her. She heard the sound of metal moving smoothly over a hard surface. As it got closer, she could see intricate engravings, constellations, like the maps that Solas was reading the night before at dinner. She smiled.

'Stop the ball, Delores,' said Oddvar.

'How?'

'Push it back with your thoughts. Force it away.'

Delores watched as the ball got closer. She could hear a ringing, as if it had a small bell inside, like one a kitten would wear around its neck. She wanted it to be closer, to see the stars and planets, listen to the bell.

'Resist the ball, Delores.'

As it got closer still, Delores believed the ball was really there, hovering in the air in front of her. She kept her eyes shut, desperate not to break the spell. She reached up to touch it. She wanted to feel the cool metal against her skin.

'Resist it, Delores Mackenzie,' urged Oddvar. But still she reached out. She touched it with her index finger, and it exploded into a burst of light. A sharp pain ran down her finger and up into her shoulder. When she opened her eyes, her finger felt like it was burning and there was a blister on its tip. She put it in her mouth and glared at Oddvar.

'Your curious facial expressions are of no consequence to me,' said Oddvar. 'I did think you would do a little better, even as a novice. No matter.' He took a key from his waistcoat pocket and opened the wooden box. Inside was a silver ball, identical to the one he'd conjured up in Delores' mind. He held the ball in his hand for a moment, as if weighing it, his long fingers and dark nails wrapped around it like spider legs. He placed the ball on the table.

'The ball inside your head was a mere thought, an illusion similar to those Prudence manifests. This ball exists here, in the physical world. It represents forces outside of your physical and psychic self. You will discover by practice that the principal is the same for illusions and the uninvited dead as it is for physical objects. I will not always be available to place images in your mind so you must take responsibility for your own development, hone your skills to their most elegant form. Do you follow?'

Delores shrugged. 'Kind of.'

Oddvar wagged his finger at her but his expression

stayed soft. '*Kind of* will not suffice. Consider these deathly visitors to be tourists in your life. Deny them the psychic energy that draws them to you and they will remain mere observers. They will watch for a while and then pass through. Allow them to draw power from you and you invite them into your reality, to walk freely in this world. You must use your skills to push the *uninvited* away, reject it, lock it out.'

Oddvar rolled the ball towards Delores. She stopped it with her hand.

'Why didn't you just use this in the first place?' she asked.

'Well what fun would there be in that for me? Take the ball and practise when you can.'

Delores saw a twinkle in Oddvar's eyes and the flicker of a smile on his thin pink lips. Maybe there was a good side to him after all.

'Thank you for the food. I know I've got a lot to learn,' she said.

Oddvar tilted his head and Delores felt his gaze was a little intrusive. She shook the feeling off.

'So, can I be excused dinner tonight? It's all a bit much. I promise I'll practise instead. In my room.' *With those dolls staring at me.*

Oddvar's concentration seemed to break at the exact moment Delores thought of the dolls and his usual unreadable expression gave way to curiosity. There was an unbearable pause and just as Delores was about to give in to pressure of speech, Oddvar broke the silence.

'Quite so, my dear. Just this once.'

Delores returned to her room with the silver ball, fully intending to practise for hours – anything to get on top of Prudence's tricks. But then she saw the soft quilt on her bed and the exhaustion she felt from the day's events soaked through every inch of her. The light was fading, and the rumbling of the cars over the cobbles outside took on a soporific rhythm. Even the dolls looked harmless. Maybe she'd imagined it all. Maybe it was Prudence. Maybe she just didn't care any more. Her eyelids were too heavy to resist any longer.

Delores was pulled back from a thick dragging sleep by a gentle, metallic humming. A rustling. A tap-tapping on the wooden floor. When she opened her eyes, the dolls were gone from the bed.

Delores lay still for a moment, needing to know where the dolls were, but not wanting to look. There was a tap-scrape-tap on the floorboards. Delores got up and knelt on the other bed, leaning slowly over the far side, trying to control her movement, dreading what she might see.

The floor came into view beyond the edge of the bed. Her mouth dried and her own rapid breathing dampened down her awareness of her gently prickling skin, registering it as little more than a fearful shiver.

The tatty-headed dolls were moving in ones and twos around a doll lying prone on the floor, a doll wrapped in a black cloak and hood, wearing the missing bird skull in place of its head. Her precious bird skull had been Frankensteined into a tiny, mutant plague doctor. Instant fury.

Prudence.

It had to be Prudence, messing around inside her head.

Delores closed her eyes and tried to push the thoughts of the dolls away. Reject them, just like Oddvar had told her. Reject the illusion. Reject Prudence.

Tap, tap, scrape.

A distant laugh.

In this room.

But not.

Delores opened her eyes again.

'Oh, thank God,' she whispered as she caught a flash of yellow sleeve, a suggestion of long brown hair. 'Maud, is that you?'

The dolls dropped to the ground and Delores flopped back onto the bed, swamped by exhaustion once more. The relief didn't last long. It was replaced by a nagging thought, an insistence that she must think again. Think differently.

The Bòcain had watched her play when she was little. They kept her company, they even moved a few things around before they were banished from the cottage, but nothing like this. They'd wanted in on *her* life, they'd wanted a way back through *her*, but Maud? Maud didn't. Maud was acting as if she were still present in her own life. Playing her own game.

Delores struggled with the thought, struggled with the razor-fine difference between the two manifestations. She didn't know if what she was thinking was even possible. Was there another state? Another step between life, the undead and the final acceptance of death? And where, exactly, was Maud?

9

Cook was back. Not that you would know it if it wasn't for the meals, drinks and snacks that magically appeared at the dining table, at the shop counter and next to Delores' bed. A small bowl of sugared almonds and a glass of warm cinnamon milk greeted her every evening, as well as a hot water bottle placed in the centre of her bed. The room was still cold, and the lanky doll still glared at her, but it didn't seem quite so grim.

'I'm not going anywhere, so get used to it,' she told the dolls. They didn't answer; they just waited for Maud.

Delores made a game out of trying to spot Cook. It felt like a great diversion and an excuse to rest her brain from all things undead. Gabriel refused to join in. He said he'd tired of that game ages ago and just to be happy she was back, if indeed Cook was a 'she'. Delores had questioned Oddvar about it but he'd simply smiled and tapped the side of his nose, and fallen asleep with a book in his lap, exhausted from the night's searches. She thought about coming clean about Maud, but what would she tell him? She didn't fully understand it herself. She weighed the thought against the risk of being sent away, and said nothing.

Bartleby shrugged when asked about Cook and Solas ignored the question. The pile of dishes left in the sink every night was washed and freshly stacked by morning. Delores had crept back down late a few times to try to catch Cook at it, but she was always too early, too late or had fallen asleep on the floor by the time it happened.

Cook's return also meant an extra half hour in bed in the morning. Delores had located the shared bathroom and was happy to allow Prudence to shower first so that the bathroom was warm with steam. Prudence was as particular about her hygiene as she was about her clothes, so the bathroom was always sparkling and ready to use. Delores never risked going after Gabriel. She was kind of sure it'd be fine, but she wasn't schooled in the habits of boys.

Days passed and Delores began to fall into a routine.

Maud was still around but not all of the time and mainly in Delores' room. If Delores was upset, angry, excited, happy, Maud would be clearer, like she was feeding off Delores' energy. She would become more substantial, and Delores could make out the details of her face, her blue eyes, and her home-chopped fringe. The physical sensations Delores had when Maud was around were unusual. She still got the prickling on her skin that announced Maud's arrival, but then she would feel calm. If Maud put her hand on Delores' arm, it was no longer cold, not warm exactly but closer to comfortable. Not death, but not life either, and the absence of the sinister Bòcan allowed Delores to relax a little into her new life. Maud would sit crossed-legged on the floor of their bedroom and they would roll the silver ball to each other. At first Delores rolled it with her hands, but after a couple of days she could gather her focus and make the ball move without touching it. She told the ball it was uninvited, will it to move and then start a pushing that originated somewhere deep in her stomach, moved up through her chest and into her thoughts. Sometimes she pushed too hard, and the ball would skid and skip back towards her, fun in a way, but Delores was aware of how undesirable that back-skip would be if she were dealing with an overly grabby Bòcan.

With each practice, the pushing was smoother, more directed. It was only a few centimetres at first, much to Maud's amusement, but by the end of a week Delores could get the ball to roll enough for the bell inside it to tinkle.

While they played Delores tried to get Maud to talk, but Maud would just shake her head and put a finger to her lips. If there was a noise on the stairs, a bird at the window or shouting in the street, Maud would be startled. She'd retreat towards the clock tower, her back against the door, and evanesce. It was clear to Delores that Maud was in hiding and she was fairly sure it was to do with the Bòcan that had shown up at the bookshop and the gallery.

Delores replayed the events in her head, trying to find a link, working out what the connection was to Maud. Just when it seemed clear, the solution slipped away again, leaving a heavy feeling in its place. Her continued attempts to ask Maud about it had ended with a smashed plate, some gut-wrenching sobbing and several more retreats to the clock tower. Whilst it had been over a week since the episode in the gallery, and practising with Maud was diverting, Delores' mind still wandered to the sinister Bòcan. Much as she wanted to dismiss it, the thought that it had been much too insistent, much too physical to give up that easily plagued her whenever the daily routine allowed her some thinking time.

Mornings were set aside for 'normal' lessons, each student taking a turn in the shop at the front. Oddvar taught the standard curriculum stuff for two solid hours at the dining table. No breaks, no conversation, which was fine. It meant Delores could avoid engaging with Prudence. The lessons that took place later, at the back of the bookstore, were much more interesting. Uncle Solas would select various texts each day, with the assistance of his darling Prudence, by far his favourite pupil.

The books were heavy with age and touched by the Uncles with such reverence that it made Delores' mouth water to imagine what it would feel like to have unfettered access to them. There were several magical books ranging from ones less than a century old on the history of witchcraft and magic, through to the much older, darker texts dealing with the conjuring and controlling of demons. Amongst them was a book that Delores suspected came from Notre Dame, along with Bartleby: *The Compendium of Demonology and Visitants*. It was a particular favourite of Oddvar's and, each time he touched it, he recounted the 'Angels for Demons' comment, smiling to himself as if it were the first time that he'd thought of it. The compendium was kept in a glass case, only to be touched by the Uncles. It was bound in black leather and fastened with two enormous silver clasps, always highly polished. The title page was adorned with skeletons and the warning *Noli me tangere* – do not touch me.

The books would be arranged on Oddvar's table, ready for him to teach from, translating as he went. The students invited to attend the sessions were to listen and remember, no notes were to be taken and there was always a strong chance of verbal quiz. Oddvar made it clear that he selected information from the texts on the basis of historical value, and would never be so irresponsible as to read a conjuring out loud. The raising of a demon, he took care to point out, would be most inconvenient. He had then given a dry little laugh, raising a rose-pink silk handkerchief to his lips. 'We are a little *removed* from the diabolic dabblers of Paris, are we not?' he joked. Delores had laughed along in nervous agreement, her mouth feigning shared merriment, the rest of her face not laughing at all.

The books were always accompanied by a small serving of treats for each student. The content of Delores' bowl varied at first. She adored the cherries dipped in dark chocolate and the tooth-achingly sweet chunks of crunchy honeycomb. She wasn't so keen on the powder-covered Turkish delight that Prudence favoured or Gabriel's Saltskalle – salty, skull-shaped liquorice sweets imported from Sweden that left you gasping for water. After only a few test runs, Cook had figured it out and each bowl that was set aside for Delores was an offering of pure joy, but she made sure to save hers for when Prudence was working in the shop.

After an encounter with Prudence, most customers were sure they would never return to the Tolbooth Book Store, but they couldn't quite figure out why. Prudence wasn't rude or unhelpful, it was just an idea planted firmly in their minds that it would not be safe to ask her a second time for something *popular* to read on the train, or for *that one by that celebrity*. Prudence would hand the customers their purchases and they would leave the shop with their new book hiding in its paper bag. The book would sit there, cuckoo-like, until the moment they fancied a light read and removed it from its wrapping. They would then be surprised to find a book by a writer 'pre-approved' by Prudence, selected from her own personal favourites, ranging from Atwood to Zusak, and each accompanied by a small note.

Your brain and your soul will thank me one day.
Regards,
Prudence S-Dottir

Delores did wonder what the 'S' stood for but, any opportunity she gave Prudence to feel superior was always snatched and thrown back at her with gusto. It was a minor mystery that could wait its turn. She watched from the joining doorway with grudging admiration as Prudence pulled this trick once more and returned the book she'd switched to the top of the freestanding table.

'Nice work,' said Delores, trying out a friendly smile as Prudence whipped round to face her. She realised it was a mistake as a sigh of disgust left Prudence's mouth.

'Don't even try, *Delores*,' she said. 'Brought your nice wee treats from Cook I see. Lovely.'

Delores spotted the twinkle in Prudence's eyes, the tightening of her mouth as she tucked a wisp of her sleek hair behind her ear.

'Cherries,' said Delores. 'Go on; try it. I dare you.'

Delores felt a strange feeling deep inside her head – not a thought but a physical scratching, gentle but annoying, like a tickle in your throat that you can't quite shift. 'Oh, Prudence,' she said, 'you're slipping. I can feel you in there.'

Uncle Oddvar's lesson was about to come in handy. *Push back the thought, reject it,* he'd told her. Delores focused on the scratching sensation and dared to look down at the bowl. Chocolate-covered cherries one moment, fresh stalks sticking out of their tops, next minute covered in mould, collapsing in on themselves, steaming and hissing. The pushing wasn't working.

'Thing is, Prudence, I know what you're up to,' said Delores. 'Oddvar told me you're an illusionist. He also said that my signals are as good as yours. I know these cherries are perfect, so get out of my head and go bug someone who cares.'

The cherries were still mouldering. Delores closed her eyes and focused again on the scratching in her head. She imagined coating the scratch in honey, the way you would drown an irritating cough. When she looked again, the cherries were plump and velvety. She popped one in her mouth.

'Delicious,' she said. 'Want one?' Delores held the bowl out, but Prudence stormed past her towards the back room, knocking her hard on the shoulder.

'Watch yourself, Delores Mackenzie,' she hissed. 'I'm only getting started.'

As Prudence disappeared into the shadows, a single feather drifted to the ground.

111

Delores was about to pick it up but was distracted by Bartleby. He was in his usual spot by the door, tutting loudly as he tried to find a comfortable position while he picked at his toenails.

'Want one?' asked Delores, hoping the cherries would distract him from his unsavoury habit. She went over to the door, knelt down, and took one out of the bowl. Whatever he was picking from his feet, she didn't want it mixing with her precious treats. Bartleby considered the cherry, sniffed it and wrinkled his little pug nose. He picked up a small carved chess piece from the floor next to him and held it out to Delores. It looked like a knight on a horse, creamy coloured and comical looking.

'Veux-tu jouer?' Bartleby asked. His voice was deep and gravelly, like he needed to clear his throat.

'*Jouer*?' asked Delores. 'Don't know what you mean, sorry.'

Bartleby held the piece between his fingers and hopped it through the air. His face softened into a mischievous grin and Delores got a look for the first time at his worryingly sharp teeth.

'A game of chess? No thanks,' she said, smiling. 'Gabriel warned me about you.'

Bartleby shrugged and went back to his basket, taking the chess piece with him. Delores caught hold of the door and looked out onto the street. Not a soul in sight. A strong wind had picked up, dragging in the familiar cold Edinburgh air as the sun sat shivering behind a cloud.

'No customers for a while by the looks of it, Bartleby.' Delores shuddered and shut the door.

She watched Bartleby for a while as he clinked chess pieces up against each other in his basket, his shoulders hunched in concentration. When he eventually fell asleep, she took the silver ball from her pocket and placed it on the counter. It had annoyed her that she hadn't been able to force Prudence out of her head, so she wanted to get a bit of practice in. She leaned towards the ball and focused all of her thoughts towards moving it. The ball hesitated at first but then rolled slowly across the surface. The bell tinkled inside. She managed to slow it to a stop before it rolled off the edge.

'Is it always this quiet?' she grumbled, but Bartleby was already snoring. She took a book from Prudence's secret stash under the counter and was soon immersed in short stories with dark edges and dubious characters.

A shadow passed beneath the shop door. It caught Delores' attention as it stretched its way across the floor. She wondered if it was a trick of the low

Edinburgh light and tried to dismiss the uneasy feeling that was building inside her. She looked more closely at the shadow, waited for it to move on. It inched closer and Delores' thumbs prickled where they made contact with the pages of her book. She closed it and placed it gently on the counter top.

'That you, Maud?' she whispered, but she knew Maud wasn't there. She couldn't *feel* her.

The bell inside the ball tinkled and the ball started to spin, tilting on the sharp edge of the counter.

Delores felt a sharp prickling at the back of her neck. It wasn't light like it was with Maud; it felt like needles jabbing in and out of her skin. Each prickling injected an uneasy mix of dread and agitation, that squirming sensation again. The temperature in the shop plummeted and her breath formed feathery white wisps.

Something was in the shop with her. Delores caught it at the edge of her vision. There was a flicker of movement to her left. It disappeared, then flickered again to her right. It slowed, and as it did Delores could make out a tall, slender Bòcan that buzzed a little around its edges. It pressed itself slowly into the shape of a woman and Delores watched transfixed as the centre of its face took form. The swirling greyness melted back into its skull, revealing pale, pearlescent

114

skin, full bright-red lips and dark eyes dusted with thick grey powder. Sweeps of black eyeliner reached towards perfectly arched brows and tendrils of chestnut hair fell across its shoulders. The centre of the Bòcan was more detailed than Delores had ever experienced, but the edges were still frayed and uncertain.

The Bòcan brushed down her coat trying to dislodge the lacework of spider webs that adorned it, knocking several fat-bodied spiders loose. Her hand was perfectly formed when brushing the central panel of the coat but faded again at the inconstant, swirling edges of her form.

Delores searched for a voice, the same way she heard Maud, but it wasn't there. Fear bloomed in the pit of her stomach as the Bòcan moved closer and opened her mouth as if to speak. Delores always had to search for Maud's voice and catch it in a half-listening, on the edge of an echo. It was gentle, passive. The sharpness of the needle-pricking in her neck, the physical memory of the pain in her shoulder at the gallery, the detail in the Bòcan's face all whispered *be afraid*. When her gaze drifted down, Delores saw the same boots that she had seen at the door, the same boots from the gallery: black with red poppies. Lady Barguest. Or had been. Once.

The boots clicked on the stone floor as she approached Delores and a thin velvet covering of hoar frost moved along in front of her feet. The same frosting appeared on the insides of the windows, giving the shop an eerie mid-winter light. Her long coat swished as she moved and the brilliantly coloured stitching of the birds that adorned it was dizzying. The closer she came the more detail emerged, and her edges became sharper, more defined. Delores felt a dragging feeling, a hollowing out, as the figure of Lady Barguest evolved.

Delores tried to move but her hands were firmly planted on the counter, pressed into place by an invisible force so heavy that her skin blanched and each tiny bone threatened to snap under its weight.

The silver ball kept spinning. Delores heard the bell hit the inside wall of the ball as it increased in speed. The planets carved on its surface blurred into one, single metallic light. The Bòcan leaned on the counter and put her face close to Delores. The light from the ball illuminated her cheekbones and cast her eyes back into their shadowy sockets. Delores switched to mouth-breathing, fearing the sweet-rot cocktail of esters that occasionally accompanied the reluctant dead if they got too close. But all she could smell was peppermint tinged with sulphur.

The Bòcan nodded towards the door that joined

the bookstore to the room at the back. It creaked shut and the lock clicked into place.

Oddvar called from the back room. 'Open the door, would you, Delores my dear?'

Delores thought about calling out to him, but the Bòcan put her finger to her lips and winked.

'Lady Barguest,' whispered Delores.

The Bòcan opened her mouth to reply, but no words came. Her eyes grew wider as her mouth moved, and she inched closer to Delores' face. There was a noise building deep inside the Bòcan, the buzzing of flies. She rounded her lips and then pulled them back over her teeth, fighting to form the words, then pressed them together again, 'M-m-m-m-m...' Then silence.

And stillness.

The Bòcan's eyes flicked to the side, towards the corner of the room. 'C-c-c-c-come out, come out wherever you are,' she hissed, her face transforming with grim delight at the sound of her own voice, still edged by the buzzing of thousands of tiny wings. She snapped her attention straight back to Delores. 'Give. Maud. Back.'

'She's not mine to give.' Delores turned her head to the side as the Bòcan leaned closer still.

'She. Is. Mine.'

Those words. That sound. The knife-sharp metallic edge of the whisper.

Delores tried to control her panic, to fight the return of the marrow-deep ache that she'd felt in the gallery. 'You're the murderer,' she whispered, 'from the painting.'

The Bòcan placed a finger on the silver ball, stopping it spinning. 'Lady Angelica Barguest. Angel.' The Bòcan tilted its head. 'Yessss. Call me Angel.' There was another flurry of excitement in Angel's face as the words fell into sentences. The flurry made Delores feel faint, weaker.

Delores looked over towards the joining door. She could hear Prudence's tetchy voice, as she rattled its handle from the other side. Then the familiar tactic, scratching around in Delores' brain.

'Not now, Prudence,' groaned Delores.

Angel followed her glance towards the back room. 'Contain them. I get – angry.'

A glance over her shoulder told Delores that Prudence's plan to get the door open was underway. A classic Prudence-shaped illusion in the form of smoke billowing from under it.

'Stop it, Prudence,' muttered Delores, but Prudence still niggled away inside her head, planting distressed voices, coughing, choking. Every detail

Prudence added got in the way of Delores gathering the focus she needed to push Angel back to where she belonged. If she was going to succeed, she'd have to deal with Prudence first.

She closed her eyes and pictured Prudence in the smoke as she dumped a bucket of water over her head. She heard a shriek and when she looked down, the smoke had gone.

Angel clapped her hands: two short, sharp claps in Delores' face. 'Brava!'

Delores flinched, in spite of herself. 'Maud isn't here.'

Angel's eyes flickered sharply to the side again. To the same corner. She held her hand up to her chin in fake puzzlement. Her hands were pale and slender and she wore a gold ring, heavy with rubies, on her wedding finger. She caught Delores looking at it and held it out in front of her, tilting her hand this way and that, admiring the ring. 'Wedding ring,' she said, and ran her other hand over it, her fingers passing through the gold and rubies. 'Gone now. Just. Like. My babies.' Angel choked on the last two words. 'All. *Dead*. Dead as … my Maud.'

'Maud isn't yours.'

'She. Will be. Soon.'

'Get out,' said Delores.

Angel's face darkened, her eyes became deeper set and something about her face shifted, like gossamer rippling over bone.

'Return what is mine.'

Delores took a deep breath, hoping to iron any signs of fear out of her voice. 'I don't have anything of yours,' she said. 'Leave now or I'll call for Oddvar.'

Angel reached for Delores' wrist, squeezing it, drawing the energy to speak. Her grip was solid and deathly cold. 'Call him in,' said Angel. 'Let him see me. Here. Because of you. The veil between the living and the dead has been stretched thin. You let me back through. And now I can get her. The rest of her. What. Would Oddvar. Do?'

'He'd get rid of you.'

'Easier get rid of *you*.'

Delores felt the doubt drop into her gut. Oddvar wouldn't be the first to dispose of her.

'Why would he do that?' she asked, trying to cover the hesitant note in her voice. 'You're the one who shouldn't be here.'

Angel laughed then slowly shook her head. 'Poor. Deluded. Delores.' Angel squeezed Delores' wrist tighter, drawing strength from her to power her voice. '*Most dangerous of gifts*. Formal containment. Psychic jail. Locked up inside your own head. He can do that. Ask him. If you dare.' Angel put her lips against Delores' ear. The smell of peppermint and sulphur were infused with the sweet rot she feared, but Delores couldn't pull back, no matter how hard she tried. 'But *I* could visit you,' whispered Angel. She let go and stood straight. A snapping movement. Too sharp.

Gabriel's comments about Oddvar and his worries about the Adjustment Council flooded back into Delores' head. Being sent away might not be the worst of it after all. She had to deal with Angel without Oddvar, and she had to start here.

'Leave. Leave now,' said Delores.

Delores focused on the idea of pushing Angel away, forcing her back across the line into the shadows where she belonged. She saw Angel slip back and for a moment she felt she might just be able to do it. She pushed again and Angel's facial features flickered, but she leaped forward instead, slamming her hands on the counter. She laughed in Delores' face.

'I WILL NOT GO INTO THE DARK AGAIN!' The words boomed up through Angel's body and out of her mouth, blasting Delores' hair back from her face. But even as Angel's demonic breath rippled her skin against her cheekbones, Delores could feel all of her focus, a channelling of her signals at last.

'Get out!' she screamed. 'Leave. You have no place here.'

The laughter stopped as suddenly as if Delores had slapped her. Angel's face adjusted itself back into place, resting on its bones, her lips red and her skin pearlescent once more. She reached into her pocket and took out a calling card. She placed it on the counter. Delores picked it up without thinking, without questioning its form.

Angel smiled. 'Good. Good,' she said. 'You have something I love and something I need. Bring them to me. Or suffer.'

Angel raised her right arm and clicked her fingers. There was a scattering of her outline as she turned to grey and evanesced.

Delores slumped forward onto the counter. The lock on the joining door clicked and it swung opened. Oddvar was waiting on the threshold. 'A moment of your time please, Delores.' There was a quiver in his voice. Delores wasn't sure if it was anger or fear. As Oddvar stepped back into his room, Prudence stayed in the doorway for a moment, smirking as she smoothed down her pinafore.

'Oh dear,' she said, then followed Oddvar.

As Delores turned to go, she heard Bartleby

calling from his basket. She hesitated for a moment, but Bartleby was insistent. As she crouched down next to him, he held one of his chess pieces out to her. His hand was shaking.

'C'est pour te protéger,' he said, and then again in English: 'To protect you.'

Delores hesitated. 'Do you see them too? The dead?'

'Some. Sometimes. Je suis un démon.' Bartleby tapped one of his fingers against his chest. 'Tu sais?'

'Yes, you're a demon. Gabriel told me. I didn't realise that meant…'

'Take it.' Bartleby placed the chess piece in Delores' hand. It was only about five centimetres tall, but it was surprisingly heavy. It was the pale cream of old ivory and its meticulous, engraved markings had grown darker with age. The figure had no neck, hunched shoulders and seemed to be peering beyond Delores into the back of the room. She ran her fingernail over its comical teeth as they bit into a shield it was holding. When Bartleby saw her do that, he gnashed his teeth together and smiled.

'He does look a bit like you, Bartleby. I have to go.' She touched Bartleby's hand in thanks and put the piece in her pocket, next to Angel's calling card, then walked to where Oddvar was waiting, wondering what on earth she was going to tell him.

10

Oddvar had been gracious, comforting and gently questioning of the incident in the front shop. He had noticed how exhausted Delores looked, congratulated her on damping down Prudence's attempts to open the door and asked if she had come to any harm. He had wondered if perhaps there had been something in the shop with her; he'd heard her shouting after all and felt quite a disturbance in the air, as if a storm was coming and then somehow had disappeared into the atmosphere, taking its strange switch in air pressure with it. He had questioned the patches of frost on the floor, the footsteps towards the counter, Bartleby's distress.

Damn, thought Delores, she'd forgotten about Bartleby. She'd run her fingers over the small figure in her pocket, hoped that Bartleby would keep quiet. As she felt the soft contours of the odd little face and its sharp teeth, she felt bad for the little demon-gargoyle. She knew he'd been afraid, and she was to blame: *she* was attracting Angel; *she* was the one bringing danger to them all. She resolved to play chess with him when Angel had been dealt with, whatever Gabriel said. It wouldn't be enough, but it would be a start.

Oddvar gave Delores every chance to ask for help. His kindness was subtle and genuine. It made her want to cry, in the same way a simple hot chocolate from loving hands can when you're at your lowest point. He'd looked at her, a glimmer of a smile on his lips.

'You have nothing to tell me, Delores Mackenzie?'

Delores thought about Maud again. She couldn't risk Oddvar sending her away or locking her up before she had the chance to help her. The idea of a psychic jail terrified her. Angel had known which buttons to press.

'No,' she said, 'the door just slammed shut and when Prudence got involved, it turned into a bit of a fight, you know, between the two of us. I didn't mean to cause any problems. I don't know about the other stuff, the frost... I'm just really tired. Can I go now?'

'You can talk to me, Delores. Maybe I can help?' Oddvar watched Delores. For a moment he was perfectly still, his hands held in front of him in an attitude of prayer, his lips parted to reveal a perfect row of tightly packed teeth, slightly yellow and a tiny slither of pink tongue peeping out between them. Just like Prudence looked when she was rooting around in Delores' brain. Her attention snapped to, and she imagined slamming down a metal shop front shutter. Oddvar gave a tiny, almost imperceptible, jump. His thin eyebrows raised in surprise and his monocle dropped from his eye. He smiled a little wider.

'You do not feel ready to extend a hand in trust towards myself or Uncle Solas. I can understand that on an intellectual level. Yes, quite understandable. Now, do go and rest and perhaps consider not only your skills, but also the skills of those around you. Never underestimate one's fellow travellers.'

Delores had a sinking feeling that Oddvar knew more than she'd spoken out loud. She hesitated but he waved her away, adding, 'I will close the shop for today while we all consider our positions within this school and our community. Please leave now,' he said, but not unkindly.

Delores trudged past Gabriel's room. His door was open and she could see an orderly stack of books on his bedside table, his glasses folded neatly on top. Gabriel was sitting on the floor at the end of his bed with his eyes closed. His tarot cards were arranged into suits next to him and his left index finger was resting gently on top of one. Delores tried to see which card was holding his attention, but she was too exhausted to stay and find out.

'See you later, Gabriel,' she whispered.

His eyes stayed shut. 'Not if I hear you first!'

Delores laughed and tried to walk quickly past Prudence's room, hoping she wasn't there. Delores was in no mood for another exchange. She irritated herself by glancing in and her steps faltered. Prudence was sitting, grinning, cross-legged on her bed, her richly coloured quilt pulled tightly into shape, revelling in the joy of Delores being in trouble with Oddvar.

Prudence's room was an elaborate mixture of perfectly curated and fascinating objects. There was a lavish rug on the polished floor, madder-root red, soft and warm. The shelves were packed with books interspaced with astronomical instruments made of antique brass, or possibly more precious metals. An exquisite blue and gold print of the night skies hung over her bed and an almost identical telescope to one Delores had seen amongst Solas' things sat on her bedside table.

'Teacher's pet,' muttered Delores. She was desperate to go in and take a closer look but tutted instead, annoyed at herself for showing even the slightest flicker of interest. She sensed Prudence's smugness burgeon as she moved on, dragging her leaden legs up the stairs to her room.

Delores' room was cold, and it was too early for Cook's hot-water bottle. She took another oversized jumper from her case, put it on over her other clothes and flung herself onto her bed, saluting the dolls on the other bed as she landed. Lanky doll turned away. Delores should have been shocked. Afraid. But she was all out of shock and fear.

Something dug into her hip as she turned on her side to settle down. She reached into her trouser pocket and pulled out the small carved figure that Bartleby had given her. She traced her finger over the shield it was holding, and the symbol engraved on its surface. She placed it on the bed along with Angel Barguest's calling card. The card had looked new when Angel had given it to her: crisp white with freshly embossed lettering. Now it was brown with age and dirt, the edges thin and disintegrating. A sickening wave of exhaustion worked its way up her body, her arms fell like lead bars by her side and her eyelids forced themselves shut against all of her good intentions.

When Delores woke, it was dark. She was fully dressed but lying under the quilt, and a hot water bottle was resting next to her. The chess piece was standing guard over a ceramic bowl, larger than the usual ones. Delores hoped it would be filled with a carefully chosen snack. She was right to hope. She smiled at the spiral of miniature chocolate-chip cookies, sprinkled with pieces of pink and white marshmallow.

'Thanks, Cook,' she whispered.

She sat up and took the bowl, grateful to be eating alone. She was far too tired to deal with Prudence. She was thirsty though and the cinnamon milk was curiously absent. She put the card and the figure back in her pocket and headed towards the kitchen. When she got to the corridor on the floor below, she got a sense of how late it must be. Everything was quiet and the only thing that lit her way were the fairy lights along the wall, but they cast strange shadows, stretching her own and mingling it with a smaller one just up ahead.

'Is that you, Maud?' she whispered but there was no blur of yellow, no small hand to guide her. There was a rustling to her left from the snug that contained the nest of straw. She could just about pick out a dark shape draped over the nest and down towards the floor but couldn't make out any detail. She assumed Solas was covered in a long cloak as he slept, giving him an almost human shape. She immediately thought back to her conversation with Esme in the sweet shop but then dismissed any further thoughts as ridiculous.

When she got to the dining room, there was a figure sat at the table, silhouetted against the dying fire.

Please don't let it be Oddvar, she thought. To her relief, it was Gabriel. She sat down next to him and he pushed a mug of hot chocolate towards her.

'I guess Cook knew you were coming,' he said. He shivered and pulled his dressing gown tight around him. It was an old-fashioned-looking thing, dark, with a rope belt. He looked a bit like a monk, sitting bleary eyed in the half dark, his hair scruffy from a restless sleep.

'Thanks,' said Delores. 'What's keeping you up so late?' She gestured towards him with the bowl of cookies, but he shook his head. She shrugged and put one in her mouth, sighing as it melted on her tongue into crumbs of buttery loveliness.

'Oh, I don't know,' said Gabriel. 'Tales of you locking doors, frosting up the front shop. Maud. The thought of her, anyway. Is she … with you?'

'Not tonight. I thought she might have been in the corridor, but she didn't come through properly. Maybe because I'm so tired.'

Gabriel tapped the side of his mug with his nails. 'What happened in the shop? I mean, *really* happened. Oddvar's shaken and that takes some doing.'

Delores didn't know where to begin. She knew it would sound ridiculous and jumbled. She placed her palm flat on the table and nodded towards the back of her hand. 'Take a look.'

'Seriously? You don't mind?'

'*You* might mind once you've seen it, but I really need someone on my side.'

Gabriel hesitated for a moment and then pinned Delores' hand down with his index finger. She watched as his eyes flickered and then grew wide. When she saw the fear arrive in them, she pulled her hand away.

Gabriel looked at her, speechless.

'You OK?' asked Delores.

Gabriel shook his head. 'Who *was* that? I mean, I don't really understand the stuff about the painting, but in the shop? She looked OK at first but … what did she turn into?'

Delores examined the back of her own hand as if she might find some answers to her own questions there. 'She's a Bòcan,' she said, 'just not like any I've ever seen. She's so solid and the detail in her face, her clothes, it's incredible. It's like she was alive again, like she could control it – death I mean. She gave me something, something real. That's never happened before.'

Delores took the card out of her pocket and handed it to Gabriel. He threw it back down on the table, as if it had burned his skin.

'I got flashes of images just touching that thing. Three children. Dead.'

'Like in the painting,' said Delores.

'What does she want?'

'I have no idea, and then, almost as weird, Bartleby gave me this.' She waved the chess piece at Gabriel. 'He said it was for protection.'

Gabriel took the piece from her. 'If Bartleby gave you this, it's serious. He never gives anything away, and this is his most precious piece. Says he "acquired" it from a museum. Not sure how it's supposed to protect you though. Did that woman, thing, whatever it was … did she say anything else?'

'Just that I had something she loved and something she needed. I have no clue what she's talking about. Maud is really scared of her though. The first time she appeared at the shop door, Maud was with me. She was terrified and begged me not to let her in. Look, I'm exhausted. I'll take this up to my room, but if you can make any sense out of what I've shown you, please let me know. I could use the help.'

'What did the calling card say? I don't want to touch it again.' Gabriel shuddered.

'Angelica, Lady Barguest, Bonaly...'

'Barguest? You know what a barguest is, right?' Gabriel leaned towards Delores, but she couldn't hold his gaze. Examining her own hand again seemed a better option.

'No, never heard of it,' she said. 'What is it?'

'A barguest is a harbinger of doom, bad fortune. It's a death demon, Delores. We have to tell the Uncles.'

'No! It'll freak them out. You see how "all about the control" Oddvar is! This is *so* out of control he'll want me out of here. I can't risk it. I need to help Maud. We have to find out what happened to her, Gabriel. She's scared, I know she is ... and the barguest thing could just be a name, a coincidence, you know?'

Gabriel placed his hand on her arm. 'Ok, calm down. You'll wake Prudence and that's never a good thing.'

Delores nodded. She took a sip of her drink and another cookie. Gabriel shifted in his seat, drumming his fingers against the table. He opened his mouth as if he wanted to ask a question but then stopped and slumped further into his chair.

Delores thought she knew what he wanted to ask. 'Did ... you want to see her? Maud, I mean?'

'How? I've never seen her before, and you made out like she doesn't want me to. You're the necromancer around here, not me.'

'Fine, but you're still a Paranormal. Maybe there's a way. There're other things we could try. Combine our talents.'

Gabriel stared at her and when it dawned on him what she meant he went even paler than usual. 'You mean the hand thing? I don't know, Delores. I don't fancy taking a look at that woman again, like, ever.'

'Trust me, I wish I didn't need to see her again either so I'm with you on that one. Maybe I could just try and show you Maud next time she's with me, guide you while you tune in. With a bit of luck, we won't need the hand thing at all.'

He tapped the back of Delores' hand. 'I really hope not.' She blushed and pulled her hand away.

'There's something else. About Maud.' Delores took a sip of her drink, watching Gabriel over the top of her cup.

'Go on,' he said. 'Can't be any worse than what I've just seen.'

Delores hesitated, prompting the much wanted 'You can trust me; we're friends, aren't we?' from Gabriel.

'It's different with Maud,' said Delores. 'She's a

Bòcan, but she – isn't. It feels like she hasn't really left this side yet, like not fully...'

'Dead? We all wish that was true,' said Gabriel, 'but wishing doesn't make it real.'

They finished their drink in silence as the fire died in the hearth and then headed for their rooms, neither expecting sleep, both wary of any dreams that might bring Angel Barguest crashing back into their thoughts.

11

Breakfast the next morning went by without incident. Delores used the shutter technique that had worked so well on Oddvar when Prudence had started to root around inside her head, trying to plant her latest torment. Prudence had stifled a flinch when the shutters slammed down, but she did give a grudging nod and a smile before smoothing her hair and turning to chat with Solas. Their language was a strange one and another reason for Delores to feel a tinge of respect for Prudence – but only a tinge, and grudgingly. Solas formed several human words and mixed them with soft kronking sounds that Delores recognised from her love of corvids – ravens in particular. She hadn't noticed the human words before, just chittering, and now she wondered if she was starting to attune to Solas somehow. Solas still treated her with an indifference that she found hard to accept, but she still wanted to be his student. All things considered, she resigned herself to the fact that Oddvar was enough to deal with for now. After a standard and rather dull geography lesson plucked straight from the Normal curriculum, Delores and Gabriel were sent to open the shop.

Gabriel was just ahead. He opened the door and glanced over his shoulder at Delores. He grabbed her wrist and dragged her through to the shop, slamming the door shut behind them.

The shop was strewn with spider webs and Delores inhaled a gossamer thin one as Gabriel pulled her in.

She spluttered and pulled the sticky clinging mess from her mouth. 'Ughh! Prudence! Just cos she couldn't get me at breakfast. I'll…'

Gabriel shushed her. 'It isn't Prudence. I'm seeing it too and she knows better than to try her illusions on me. I know all her secrets and I find them every time, no matter how deep she buries them. We have a mutual understanding, me and her. We can reach out for each other, check in, but that's it. This has to have been your Barguest woman, Bòcan, whatever. We have to get rid of it and fast. Oddvar sees this and we're done. You wait here and I'll go get a couple of brooms. And check on Bartleby.' Gabriel blushed at his own rudeness. 'Please.'

The shop windows were covered in silken webs, allowing the light through but giving it an eerie silver glow, and the book spines were dulled by the same gossamer-thin lacework. A bookshop turned into a graveyard and not a single spider to be seen. A different kind of calling card, proof that Angel was never far away. Delores ran over to Bartleby's basket. He was awake, shivering and covered in dense, sticky webbing. Delores got to work, starting with the webs around his mouth and throat. The more she touched them, the more she got the sensation of Angel being somewhere close, watching her. Bartleby gasped when his mouth was clear and sat panting as Delores wiped the thinner, more delicate ones from his little horns and pointed ears. 'You OK, Bartleby?'

He shook his head, his neck creaking as he stretched his thick rigid muscles. 'She was here,' he said. 'La dame démoniaque, the evil lady. Oui, just for a moment. Searching. You have it? La protection que je t'ai donné?'

Delores shrugged, regretting her lack of attention in French classes. She'd always had another book hidden on her lap at her old school. Always the sad loser at the back of the class. 'Sorry, Bartleby,' she said, 'You'll have to speak to me in English.'

Bartleby showed his disapproval in the usual way,

but this time it looked a little half-hearted as he stuck his tongue out at her. 'The protection I gave you. The chess piece. It has a charm beyond its own beauty.' Bartleby waved his hand out in front of him, looking past Delores, reliving something she couldn't see. 'Tu comprends?'

Delores took the figure out of her pocket and offered it back to Bartleby. He wrapped his rough palm and sharp talons tenderly around her hand. 'Keep it,' he said. 'She does not want me. Je l'ai ennuyée … uhm, en anglais, huh…? I bored her. I am just an object to her, of no use. She wants you *and* the little one. The piece will help.'

'How? I don't understand,' said Delores, but Bartleby turned away. He pulled his blanket over him and as Delores stroked his shoulder, he started to snore.

Gabriel shoved a sweeping brush and some dusters through the door. 'Get cleaning and I'll keep Oddvar busy.'

'No gloves?' Delores was horrified at the thought of having to touch any more of it, as if it would somehow connect her to Angel.

'Just think of it as … I don't know, spider silk,' said Gabriel. 'Think gothic novel; you'll be fine.'

Delores started by knocking down the webs she

could reach with her duster and used the brush to reach the higher ones. Her attempts to sweep them into a pile for disposal failed. The sticky threads clung to the bristles of the brush, even when she tried to knock them off by banging the end of the broom on the floor. Delores didn't want to touch them again, but short of throwing them out of the shop door still attached to the broom onto the street, she had no choice. As she dared to touch the bristles, the sensation of Angel watching her intensified, that feeling that someone is staring at the back of your neck, willing you to turn around. She felt swathes of panic rising, but before it could escalate it was squashed by the feel of the familiar small hand on hers. In the silver half-light created by the window webs, she saw Maud's yellow sleeve.

'Please, Maud,' she whispered. 'Show yourself properly, like you do when we play. I want to help you. *We* want to help you, me and Gabriel, but he needs to know it's you. He wants to believe me; I know he does.'

Maud let go of her hand and Delores heard light footsteps, moving away towards the shadows on the far side of the shop. As she looked into the darkest corner, she saw Maud materialise, clearer than all of the times before. Her yellow coat wasn't a raincoat as Delores had thought; it was a duffle coat, thick and warm against the Edinburgh winds, her jeans were folded back into deep cuffs just above her ankles and she wore pink and white canvas shoes. Her brown hair hung loose and a little tangled over her shoulders and her cheeks were pale and rounded. Delores' heart ached when she saw Maud's eyes, dark and sunken, and her hands, still blue with cold. Maud waved and Delores did the same.

'What are you doing?' Gabriel's voice made her jump.

'Maud's here. She knows you want to see her.'

'Where? Where is she?'

'In the corner on the far side there. Can't you see anything?'

Gabriel narrowed his eyes. 'Nothing.'

'Look slightly to the side. She's standing under the book festival poster but sometimes it's best not to look directly.'

Gabriel moved his head left, then right. 'Still nothing. Can I…?' He reached for Delores' hand, but she pulled away when she saw the look of fear on his face. She didn't want that, not from him. She'd seen it before on the face of a girl that had, rarely, tried to be friends with her, and it had hurt. Deeply.

Delores had an idea. She'd left the silver ball the day before when Oddvar had summoned her. It must be in the shop somewhere and if Oddvar had cleared up after her, it would be somewhere sensible and appropriate. The safe under the counter. 'What's the combo for the safe?'

'Erm … Oddvar's birthday.'

'Which is?' Delores raised her hands in a questioning shrug.

'One, ten, ninety-eight.'

Delores sighed. 'Come on, he's older than that surely. You must have it wrong.'

'1898,' said Gabriel, 'but we don't use the 18. Too long.'

'What? That makes him like a hundred and twenty?'

'Roughly … Solas is even older. He was Oddvar's tutor way back. Not bad for a hundred and whatever-ty. You must have met some of the really old ones before?'

Delores shook her head. 'A lot of this stuff is new to me remember. I was having a pretty normal life until a couple of weeks ago.'

'Course you were,' said Gabriel.

Delores switched her attention back to the task in hand. She turned the dial and the door clicked open. The silver ball was resting on top of the brown money sack. 'Watch this,' she said.

Delores rolled the ball along the floor towards Maud. She saw Maud smile and sit cross-legged on the floor ready to play. Maud put her hand up and stopped the ball just before it reached her feet.

'Gabriel, can you see where the ball is?' asked Delores. 'Maud's just on the other side of it. She'll roll it back in a minute.'

Gabriel nodded. Maud rested her chin on her hand and stared at the ball. It rolled slowly at first, picking up speed, the bell tinkling inside. Delores held her hand up and stopped the ball before it hit her own feet. She could feel Gabriel trembling next to her. When she looked, his mouth was hanging open.

'Look I believe you, OK. She's there. Or something is. I still can't see her though. I've got no choice, have I?'

'Are you sure?'

Gabriel took a deep breath. 'Give me your hand.'

Gabriel stood close to Delores, their shoulders touching, and Delores could hear him breathing fast and deep through his nose.

Delores placed her hand on his shoulder and leaned into him. He smelled sweet, like freshly baked bread. She was shocked by a sudden attack of the blushes and visualised stamping on all of the weird and uninvited feelings that were suddenly swirling around inside her before Gabriel had any chance of spotting them. *Those ones can definitely sit inside a nicely locked box*, she told herself.

Delores nodded at Maud and Maud nodded back. 'She's saying it's OK. Looks like we have three sets of skills working together now. I'll try to block the other stuff, Angel and the children, all of that, but don't go looking for it just in case. I'm not exactly star pupil around here and there's a reason for that. Dig too deep and I might not be able to help you.' Delores felt the heat of the red blotches that constantly betrayed her, spreading across her neck. 'Only think about Maud,' she added, a little too quickly.

When Gabriel touched her hand, he gasped. Delores looked away, not wanting to intrude on what she knew would be a deeply personal moment.

'Oh my God, I can see her,' he whispered. 'It is her. It's Maud.'

12

Delores beckoned for Maud to come out of the shadows. She didn't move at first, checking around the shop, looking for something. It occurred to Delores that Maud might be able to sense Angel's presence in the remains of the webs, just like she could.

'Don't worry,' said Delores. 'She isn't here. It's just stuff she left behind.'

Maud nodded and stepped forward into the silvery light.

'Maud?' whispered Gabriel. 'What happened to you? We've looked everywhere.'

Maud looked towards the door and then back at them. She opened her mouth and it looked as if she were speaking quickly but they couldn't quite make it out. They could hear snatches of words mixed in with a crackling sound, like a bad radio signal.

'We can't hear you properly,' said Delores. 'Try speaking in single words. Like you did on the stairs.'

Maud opened her mouth and tried to force out a word, but it stuck in her throat. Her face crumpled as if she was about to cry.

'I'm sorry, Maud. We don't want to upset you,' said Delores, distressed by Maud's pain, 'but if we're going to help you, we need to know what happened.'

Maud nodded and her face settled again. She held out her hand towards Gabriel. Delores could feel him shaking next to her.

'It's OK,' said Delores. 'Maud has no reason to hurt you. I know it's hard to see her this way but please, just try to make contact with her. You said you loved her. She'll remember that. I know she will.'

'How? How do you *know* that? I mean, it looks like Maud but how do we know for sure? What if it's really Angel pretending she's Maud?'

At the mention of the word Angel, Maud put her hands over her ears and her face contorted into a scream. She looked as if she were screaming with every part of her body but only a distant, heart-breaking wail could be heard, as if it was coming from the street, or another building, anywhere but that room.

'I'm sorry, I'm sorry,' said Gabriel. 'Please, Maud, I believe it's you. Forgive me, please.'

But Maud kept screaming. Delores pulled away from Gabriel and went over to where Maud was standing but by the time she got there, Maud was gone.

'I guess she answered your question,' said Delores.

'What question?'

'About what happened? It was definitely Angel.'

A commotion in the back room startled Delores and Gabriel back into action. Prudence was shouting about wanting to be in the front shop, that something was *going on*. Oddvar was trying to calm her but they both knew it wouldn't be long before Prudence got her own way and stormed through.

They pulled the webs down from the windows as best they could and used the brooms to clean the frames. Gabriel unlocked the shop door and lifted Bartleby into place. Bartleby was still shivering so Gabriel wrapped his blanket around his shoulders and whispered, 'Please, Bartleby, whatever you saw, keep it to yourself for now, I'm begging you.' Bartleby pushed the tip of his tongue through his teeth but thought better of it. He nodded, pulled his blanket a little tighter and went back to sleep just as the first footfall of people in the street moved past.

Delores had taken both brooms outside and was crouching at the edge of the pavement, disposing of a tangle of webs when Prudence finally burst through the door.

'Glad to see you're finally in the gutter where you belong, *Delores*,' she shouted.

Delores waved a hand signal that was open to interpretation and came back into the shop.

'I know something's going on,' said Prudence. 'Oddvar was trying to tune into something, and he almost had it, said he'd felt a psychic shift. He was shivering. Tried to hide it by putting on his best silk cravat but I could tell he was upset.'

'Then what was all the shouting about,' asked Delores, leaning up against the brooms.

'I had to distract him; he was about to come through. It was tempting to let him, but I was curious. I know what a snake you are, Delores. You'd have managed to get sent to your room to "consider your skills", again. Plus, I'd never drop Gabriel in it. If there's anything interesting going on around here, the least you could do is include me.'

Gabriel looked at Delores, then back at Prudence. 'Well…'

'Nothing! Not anything to do with you anyway,' said Delores. Gabriel jumped at the sharp interruption and Prudence smirked at his obvious discomfort.

'Really?' she said. 'When you realise you need someone with a proper brain, you know where to find me.'

Prudence turned away and then paused, her back to Delores and Gabriel. 'I heard you mention Maud, and if I did, so did Solas.'

Once he was sure Prudence was gone, Gabriel rolled his eyes and then slumped across the counter. 'She's right. About Solas. He'll be thinking about what he's heard, working out what to do about it. It's what he always does. He owes a lot to Oddvar...'

'Like what?' asked Delores.

'It's complicated, like *really* complicated. They protect each other, and Prudence.'

'See, there you go again,' said Delores. 'Prudence, Prudence, Prudence. I know she's upset, but you're upset, Bartleby's upset, *everyone* here is upset. What is so special about Prudence flipping S-Dot whatever-it-was?'

'You should pay more attention to names,' said Gabriel. 'We need to focus. Maud's who I care about right now, the rest can come later, but Solas will involve Oddvar in anything that might bring the authorities down on us, and with good reason.'

The mention of Solas made Delores uneasy, and not just because Oddvar was already suspicious. It was what Sweet-Shop-Esme had said. Delores was sure there was some mix up, but the questions about Solas hadn't gone away, they'd simply taken a back seat.

'Just give me something, please, Gabriel, so I can try to make sense of things. What's all this threat from the authorities? Why would Solas care if I was sent somewhere else? He hates me anyway.'

'Fine. You must have noticed he's not *just* a bird. I don't know exactly how it works, but all of the Uncles have some animal connection. Some more so than others. Solas is definitely more.'

'Does he ever … take another form? I mean, I know that's impossible, it's just something I heard.'

'You been chatting to Sweet-Shop-Esme by any chance?'

Delores nodded.

'Hmmm. Solas isn't always discreet…' Gabriel looked away '…and not always a bird.'

'A shapeshifter? I thought the Council had rounded all of those up?'

'*Those?*'

Delores blushed. 'Sorry.' She gestured for Gabriel to continue.

'Solas owes Oddvar a *lot*, so if you really want to help Maud before you get rumbled, time's running out. What's the plan?'

'Plan? When I have one,' said Delores, 'you'll be the first to know.'

13

Delores decided she'd take her lunch to Princes Street Gardens. She needed some air, some space to make the connections that always felt marginally beyond her grasp at the Tolbooth. Most of all, she needed to be away from other people's prying thoughts.

The weather had brightened and, with a couple of extra layers on, Delores knew she'd be fine. She didn't want to give anything away before she'd decided what to do, who to involve. The thought that Angel could show up whenever she felt like it was also weighing heavily on her mind. Angel's last visit had left a feeling of disquiet behind amongst the cobwebs.

Delores went back to her room to get her things. She pulled her backpack from under her bed for the first time since her arrival at the Tolbooth. It felt heavy and thudded as Delores dropped it against the floor. The book. How could she have forgotten it? It would be a great lunch companion – better than having one of Prudence's illusions in her head. Delores had felt like Edgar Allan Poe was her only friend, until Gabriel. From *The Tell-Tale Heart* to *The Raven*, his words had never let her down.

As Delores lifted the book to put it back in her bag, a familiar ache ran down the muscles in her arms, a discomfort tugged at her stomach. The same feelings that she'd had when she'd held the book that last day in her room at the cottage in Cramond. Maybe it *was* just guilt, she thought.

Delores reached for the calling card and slipped it between the pages of the book. She knew Cook would be in her room at some point and she didn't want anyone else to touch it. Everyone else at the Tolbooth was a Paranormal, so it would make sense if Cook was too. She put the chess piece in her pocket and headed downstairs.

Oddvar was studying in the dining room as Delores made her way towards the front door.

'Please do not leave without your lunch, Miss Mackenzie. Cook would be most offended and somewhat concerned for your wellbeing.'

Delores approached the table. Steam rose from

Oddvar's delicate china cup and next to it was a plate of sandwiches, stuffed to spilling with odd-shaped leaves, stems and small purple flowers. He was reading but held a fruit knife and a peach to one side. His fingers worked deftly to slice the tender flesh, and his black nails were shiny with juice that dripped conveniently into a small copper receptacle. Oddvar didn't glance once at the peach or Delores. He nodded towards a white paper bag on the table.

'Take it, please. I will not have Cook distressed by a lack of appreciation,' he said. 'I have added a session with Uncle Solas to your schedule this afternoon. It is time to break the ... what is it now? Ahh yes ... ice.'

Delores' heart sank. 'How am I supposed to do that when I can't understand a word he says?'

'Come now, the occasional word is surely filtering through. Consider it an opportunity for a higher level of learning.'

Oddvar cleaned his fingers on his napkin and ran them along the golden edges of the pages. Delores noticed his hand was trembling. 'You may thank Cook by ensuring you eat all of the meal provided, and me by returning promptly at two. You are now free to leave.'

Delores headed for the western end of Princes Street Gardens. The noise of the fountain there was calming and the golden paint always gave the air a warmer light to read by. The grassy bank was damp and cold, so she sat on one of the insanely uncomfortable wooden benches. She arranged her lunch next to her to discourage any company and took out the book. The ache in her arms returned, but she could ignore it for a little alone time with her favourite writer.

But as Delores opened the front cover, the ache intensified. A shadow moved across the end papers obscuring her view. A bird maybe? She looked up and caught sight of a Bòcan sitting in the upper bowl of the tiered fountain. It startled her at first, but it was only lightly formed, nothing more than a shadow where one shouldn't exist. The sight of the water running through its will-o'-the-wisp legs was strangely reassuring. Definitely watching her, but thankfully not Angel. She looked back to the book to discourage the minor apparition from coming any closer, but it had alerted her to the fact that her signals were still out there, still attracting random ghouls and over-stayers.

Any relief she'd felt at realising it was just a standard Bòcan was shattered as she read the book's title page. How could she have forgotten the inscription? It had seemed so charming when she first took the book from the school library but now it chilled her to her core.

To my darkest Angel, my Lady of the tower

'Angel,' she whispered. She flipped through the pages to find the calling card and then placed it against the inscription. The card read *Angelica, Lady Barguest, Bonaly Towers.* 'Lady of the tower.' The hairs on her arms stood up like pins and her neck was cold and clammy. The hint of peppermint that suddenly appeared on the air was cut through by an unmistakeable voice.

'You called?'

Delores looked to her left and Angel was sitting next to her, amongst a blanket of frost that crept over the back of the park bench. A patch of daffodils that had been growing by the leg of the bench had withered and died and Delores' sandwiches were strewn across the grass, ground into the dirt.

'Oh dear,' said Angel. 'Were those yours?'

Delores was startled by the clarity of Angel's voice, the regularity of her speech pattern. She was vivid. Present. Delores thought back to the moment at the Tolbooth when Angel grabbed her wrist. The sapping feeling, the way Angel brightened. It worried Delores to think where Angel was drawing her power from now. She hoped it wasn't Maud. There was so little of her left.

'But look here,' said Angel. 'You seem to have

remembered one of the things you have of mine.' Angel gestured towards the book.

'If it's so important to you,' said Delores, 'take it and go back to wherever you came from. I'm assuming Hell's not such a wild guess, or that general postcode.' Delores closed the book and held it in front of Angel. Angel's hand moved towards it and then pulled back.

'I don't quite seem to have the strength … yet.'

Angel's dark eyes widened, and her skin pulled back against her skull, the way it had at the Tolbooth when the polite façade had begun to slip. Her teeth became more prominent and showed signs of extreme decay. Her black glossy tongue washed across them, leaving them smeared with grey. The peppermint in the air gave way to sulphur and Delores put her hand over her mouth and nose.

Angel leaned in towards the book and although Delores wanted to run, she could only manage to lean away in equal measure. Angel almost had her face against the book's cover. She breathed deeply through her nose, inhaling its scent, then pulled back. She smiled at Delores and her face took its more acceptable form. Angel smacked her newly red lips.

'How lovely to be near it again,' she said. 'Such a wonderful token of love. Eternal loyalty. Wouldn't you say? I will have it back when the time is right, when

I am fully in my power again. But for now it suits me for you to keep it. It binds us together. Bring it to me, along with the thing I need.'

The dragging feeling through Delores' arms felt like toothache, it was pulling at her so hard it was getting difficult to concentrate. She struggled to get the words out. 'I don't know what you mean.'

'Little Maud, she does hide from me so. And now she seems a little … stuck in between. You must bring her to me.'

'I'd never give you Maud.'

'Never? Are you sure?' Angel leant forward, one elbow on her knee and her knuckle under her chin. Her skin sparkled in the light, and her cheeks were rounder. There was a smile on her lips, but her eyes remained dark, dead. Delores was relieved that the scent of peppermint was stronger again, but the back-note of sulphur was still there.

'You like him, don't you?' said Angel.

'Who?'

'That other *angel* in your life. The blond boy. Quite charming, for a divinatory. They're normally rather annoying and unbearably smug. Little know-it-alls.'

Delores didn't realise until that moment that it was possible to be frozen with fear and feel the heat of embarrassment at the same time.

'How very sweet,' said Angel. 'A blush on such a delicate flower.' She put her hand out, reaching to brush Delores' cheek with her finger. Delores pulled back. 'Such a shame,' sighed Angel, putting her head to one side and pouting her lips.

'What do you mean?'

Angel laughed, covering her offence. 'Don't you see it? My form, my face, my hands? Am I not more beautiful? Am I not more present in this life? How could that have happened? It's as if I've got some extra energy from somewhere, a little smattering of life-force. Do run along, Delores, before you're too late. You really should keep a better eye on your friends; don't leave them unattended for too long. When you have pieced together our little puzzle, come and find me. Bring the thing I love and the thing I need. Do it quickly and your charming divinatory may live yet. Let's say no more about it, precious lamb. You're wasting time.'

Angel stood and walked towards the fountain, disappearing into the sunlight that filtered through the spray of water. She took the gnawing ache with her. Delores grabbed her things and ran back to the Tolbooth.

14

Prudence was behind the counter and wasn't even halfway through her latest insult when Delores pushed past her. Gabriel wasn't in the back room either, just Oddvar. He held his hand up to stop her.

'What can be so important? Other than the fact that you are over an hour late?'

'I can't be,' panted Delores. 'I was hardly gone. Where's Gabriel?'

'Gabriel is resting. He was taken quite unwell earlier. We think he may have been doing a reading and over-taxed himself. Those delightful cards were quite scattered about the doorstep. Antique of course, the cards. Minimal damage. Just a boot print and an echo of some psychic activity. A chill in the air, so to say.' He paused long enough for Delores to offer comment. She didn't. She was putting all of her energy into guarding her face against any expression that might give her away.

'And?' she snapped. 'What are you doing about it?'

'Manners, *please*,' said Oddvar, as if Delores' words were causing him physical pain. 'We took him to his room. A doctor from within our own ranks has been contacted and will attend. You must go immediately and apologise to Solas for your lateness. He is in his own corner studying upstairs; you may sit with him there.'

'Suits me fine,' muttered Delores as she pushed past.

'Stop,' said Oddvar. He didn't shout it, the word was barely above a whisper, but his voice was sharp – not in tone but in physical impact. It was inside her head and the word rooted Delores to the spot. Oddvar moved round to look her in the eye. Delores pulled down her mental shutters. It didn't startle Oddvar this time but she did feel a twinge of guilt at the sadness that swept across his face.

'You *can* talk to me, Delores. I am no man's fool, nor any child's fool for that matter. You may find me more understanding than you think. I sense a fear within you, and you are not used to that fear. You are familiar with sadness, are you not? Such deep, consuming sadness. But the fear is new, recently planted and by a malicious hand, I fancy.'

Delores focused on the shutters that she had visualised to keep Oddvar out, but they were thinning, bending as if Oddvar was turning them to fabric. She channelled her energy towards solidifying them again, but she still couldn't move. Angel had been right. Oddvar could imprison her if he wanted to, and she had no idea what would happen to Maud then. She might stay stuck and afraid forever. They might never find her. Or find her body. An eternity of fear and hiding. Just when she thought she couldn't feel any worse, Prudence slid past her, smothered in satisfaction at seeing Delores in one of Oddvar's psychic locks. Delores watched helpless as Prudence slipped away up the stairs.

As suddenly as Oddvar had gripped Delores, he let her go. She staggered forward. 'I...'

'I know there was a presence in the shop with you, Delores, and it was a fearful one. I felt its darkness in the frost it left behind. The dead have no place amongst the living. Death is the end of our stay in this realm and should remain so.'

'Then what are my skills worth then? Nothing?'

'Your skills are valuable but only when you can control them. Communications, *true* necromancy, that is of use to our community. Re-embodiment of the dead is banned by our Council, and for good reason. Do not risk being taken in a Gathering, Delores Mackenzie.'

'A what?'

Oddvar paused. 'Please attend your lesson with Uncle Solas and extend your apologies as requested. You may go.'

'A Gathering? Is that what you saved Solas from? Is that what he's *so* grateful for? I know he's a shapeshifter and I know they're banned, so why isn't *he* at risk from a Gathering? You protected him, didn't you?'

Oddvar flinched. 'I am finding your *abruptness* most uncomfortable,' he said.

He waited for Delores to have the good grace to look embarrassed and then continued. 'I did indeed protect him, and I did so because he is my friend. That is what friends do, is it not? He is also a valuable asset to this school. This country's government will only tolerate a certain level of Paranormal society to exist amongst its own; the First Minister is adamant on this point. You are aware of this of course. Your own parents were taken in the last one I believe, for overstepping the supernatural bounds in a manner similar to your own.'

Delores was hit so hard by the shock of Oddvar's revelation that she didn't have time to protect herself.

'Ah,' he said. 'I see now that you were not aware. I apologise for my … indelicacy.' Oddvar pushed a chair towards Delores. Any strength she had left after her sprint back from the gardens drained from her body. She stumbled towards the chair and sat down.

'A certain level of Paranormal propriety must be maintained,' said Oddvar. 'It is a delicate balance between our own government and those of each country we inhabit.'

'Does my sister know?' whispered Delores.

'I always assumed that you were both fully aware of the situation. It is possible that she is as uninformed as yourself.'

'They said they couldn't report any trace of them. The department … they lied.'

Oddvar reached out as if to comfort her but withdrew his hand, realising swiftly that it was not welcome. 'Cannot report is quite different to cannot find, my dear.'

'But why lie?' asked Delores. 'And if they're not dead, where are they?'

'Lie? They don't see it that way. The Taken no longer exist in their eyes. There are various holding points around Europe and I believe they were sent north. Beyond that, I have no idea.'

Delores forced down the tears, the way she always

did. She'd let them fall later. In private. 'Will you help me find them?' she whispered.

'Find? What use would there be in *finding*? Contact would never be granted.' Oddvar looked away from her, his fingers fiddling with the gold chain on his monocle.

'I have a right to...'

Oddvar raised his palm to stop her. 'Be *very* careful.'

'Careful? *Careful*?' Delores could feel the rage building inside her. 'What's the use of careful if I have no one? My parents never hurt anyone; they were good, kind people. If they did anything wrong, they must have been trying to ... to...'

'Help someone? I know about Maud,' said Oddvar. 'I saw her. Not overtly, but inside your head, the day the other one came. We spoke after the events, if you recall. I cannot help Maud. I do not have the skills required to deal so directly with the reluctant dead, which is why she came to you, I suspect. If I have sensed the darker force that is drawn to you, I will not be the only one. I have not lost a student to a Gathering yet. I will not lose you or ... any other. Accept that you might not be able to help Maud. If I need to intervene, to shut you down, then I will, for the good of all of my students and for the good of this establishment.'

'Maud is your student too.'

'*Was* my student.' Oddvar paused, visibly shaken by his own words. He gathered himself quickly. 'Are we clear on this point?'

'You've given up on her.'

'Do not sit in judgement of things you do not fully understand. Do you accept this to be the end of the matter?'

Delores nodded and looked away. She arranged her thoughts quickly to prevent Oddvar from checking for her compliance, but she couldn't sense him searching her mind. He clicked his fingers and Delores was guided forward as if by an invisible hand. Oddvar returned to his table and his books. The conversation was over.

Delores paused at the bottom of the stairs. She didn't want to give Oddvar's bombshell the headspace it needed right now. She couldn't. She shut it away and headed for Gabriel's room, stepping lightly, fighting the urge to run. She willed with everything she had that Gabriel would be OK, wishing she'd find him sitting at the end of his bed with his cards as usual. She hoped if she was supremely quiet, she'd be able to sneak in without Solas knowing she was there.

While Delores stepped slowly, in those precious

moments between wishes and inevitability, she could make believe that Angel had been lying, that she had no power over Gabriel, that it had all been a trick to frighten her into doing what she was told. As she turned towards Gabriel's room, her heart sank at the sight of the slender shape of Prudence S-Dottir tapping gently on his door.

15

Prudence stopped knocking the moment she sensed Delores behind her. She opened her mouth to speak but Delores shook her head and put her finger to her lips.

'Wait,' she mouthed.

Delores crept around the corner to take a look at Solas. The low sun was coming in through the window, drenching his black feathers, transforming them to a deep indigo blue. He was sitting amongst his books on the floor with his legs drawn under him, but his eyes were open. Or at least the one Delores could see was. His head nodded slightly, as if he were dozing, and he gave no indication that he knew Delores was there. She'd read somewhere that birds can control which part of their brain was asleep, that they could literally sleep with one eye open, a defence against predators.

She stood and watched him for a few moments more to be sure. She lifted her arm slowly, then waved, but there was no recognition of her presence from Solas.

Delores crept back to Gabriel's room, opened the door and gestured for Prudence to go in. Prudence stood and glared at her so Delores grabbed her wrist and pulled her inside.

The room was dark and airless, the curtains drawn against the small window above Gabriel's bed. The lack of air should have made the room stuffy, but it was cold, much colder than the space outside his door. Gabriel's breaths were soft and regular as he lay on top of the bed covers, arms straight by his side. Sleeping but deathly still. Delores leaned over him to get a closer look. She caught the faint hint of peppermint as she wiped a silver cobweb from his hair. The cobweb stirred that familiar dragging dread in the pit of her stomach.

'What are you doing?' hissed Prudence. 'He's just having a lie down. Probably got a headache from listening to you.'

'If you truly believe that, why were you knocking on his door?' asked Delores.

Prudence wrinkled her nose up into her signature sneer. 'Because I know him better than you. I was trying to … speak to him, but he wasn't… Oh never mind. You wouldn't understand.'

'Try me,' snapped Delores. 'You don't have exclusive friendship rights.' She felt the tell-tale blotches spreading across her neck again. *Goddammit!* 'Make yourself useful at least. Open the curtains so I can get a better look at him.'

The feeble light that crept in through the thick, bubbled glass was enough to confirm Delores' worst fears. Gabriel's lips were sealed together with the same hoar frost that Angel had deposited in the shop just a day earlier. His face showed no expression, no dreaming. He was breathing but the essence that made him Gabriel was missing.

'What have you done, Angel?' whispered Delores.

'Ewww! Stop!' Prudence emphasised her point with some delicate fake gagging.

'What? I don't mean *him*. It's a long story, but Gabriel's not asleep. He's … I don't know exactly. You know what I do, right? My skills?'

'All that stuff about the dead?'

'Bòcain. It means…'

'I know what it means,' said Prudence. 'Me and about sixty thousand other Gaelic speakers. You really need to stop thinking you're unique. And I'd hardly call it a skill when *they* hunt *you*.' She looked back towards the bed. 'He looks weird. I'm getting Oddvar.'

'No!' Delores instantly regretted the almost-shout she let out. She looked quickly towards the door.

'I'll get Solas then. He looks almost...' Prudence couldn't bring herself to say it.

'Dead? Well, he's not. Not yet.' Delores whispered the last part, but Prudence still caught it.

'Yet? What have you done? I'm getting Oddvar. I don't care what you think.'

Delores stepped in front of the door. 'No, you're not.'

'Oh, give me a break, Delores. I don't actually have to leave the room to get in touch with the Uncles and you know it. Didn't you learn anything from my visits inside that sad little brain of yours?' She tapped her index finger against Delores' temple. Delores grabbed her by the wrist.

'Don't ever do that again, Prudence, or I swear...'

'What? What do you swear?' Prudence laughed in her face, but she took two steps back. 'I could speak to them right now and you couldn't stop me.'

'Wow, Prudence, aren't *you* just the queen of all things Paranormal.'

Prudence allowed herself a minimal smile of self-appreciation and Delores kicked herself as she watched Prudence's tiny flicker of self-doubt fade and die.

'You'd better believe it, *Delores*,' she said. 'Now move.'

Delores stepped away from the door. 'Fine. You win! Isn't that you wanted to hear? You beat me. Step inside my head, have a rummage around. Go on, do your worst! See if I care. You are victorious!'

Prudence smiled again but the smile slipped when she looked back at Gabriel. 'OK, you've got my attention.'

Delores picked a quilt from the end of Gabriel's bed and pulled it up over him. She tucked it under his chin and smoothed it down over his legs. She touched his forehead and tried not to shudder at the feel of his skin. It was so cold it made the palm of her hand ache, and her heart ache more. 'I'll tell you what's going on,' she said, 'but you have to promise you won't get the Uncles involved. Especially Solas. Exactly how much do you know about him?'

Prudence tried her usual delaying tactic. The signature smoothing of the pinafore. 'What do you mean?' she asked, examining non-existent fluff on her shoulder strap.

Delores couldn't figure out why Prudence, brutally direct in all other aspects, was so evasive about this one thing. She was missing something, something that would thread it all together. It felt like more than misguided loyalty or respect for a teacher, but she didn't have the headspace for another puzzle. 'I *mean*,' she said, 'there's something a bit off about him. Oddvar's weird, but Solas? Something's not right.'

'And what would that be, genius? Other than the fact he's a bird.' Prudence glanced off to one side. A classic tell.

'So, you do know something,' said Delores. 'The shapeshifting by any chance?'

Prudence nodded but kept her mouth firmly shut.

'Anything else?' asked Delores. 'Are you sure he's the great and righteous *bird* you seem to think he is?'

There was a flash of anger across Prudence's face. She handled it quickly, but Delores had caught it.

'I don't care whether you like my ... if you like Solas or not,' said Prudence. 'You don't know him; you don't know any of us.' Delores winced at the truth of the last part. If Prudence noticed, she regretted nothing. 'Tell me what's going on, right now,' she said, 'or I am going to the Uncles.' She perched on the end of the bed, then rolled her eyes and sighed deeply at the pause between her ultimatum and any chance Delores had had to respond.

Delores knew this was her once chance. She'd have to go in hard. 'Maud. It started with Maud.'

Prudence grabbed Delores' arm. 'What did you say?'

Delores could feel Prudence's fingers digging into her muscles and tendons. She tried to pull away, but she couldn't. Prudence was inside her head before the shutters were even halfway down. She watched as Prudence's anger turned to horror. She imagined her watching it all, the whole thing playing out like a movie: Angel, the spider webs, the demonic painting, but worst of all, Maud.

Delores wanted to be angry with Prudence for her invasion, but as despair spread across her classmate's face, she felt tears running down her own. When it became too much, Prudence let go and Delores fell back onto the floor.

Prudence put her head on her knees, covered it with her arms, and sobbed. Any anger Delores felt towards Prudence drifted away.

'I'm so sorry, Prudence,' she said. 'Gabriel wanted to tell you when Angel showed up, but I was worried you'd tell Oddvar, or Solas.' Mentioning the Uncles again triggered a niggling thought at the back of Delores' mind. Then it hit her. 'Lock the Uncles out, Prudence. Out of your head. Right now! Oddvar was trying to read me earlier and I'm sure he saw stuff. He threatened to shut me down. I can't help Maud if that happens, can I?'

Prudence stopped crying as suddenly as she'd started.

'Lock you down? Like a full-on psychic lockdown? Why would he do that? That's extreme, even for Oddvar.'

'He's worried I'll attract a Gathering. Overstepping the bounds of *Paranormal propriety*.'

Prudence looked terrified. 'A Gathering? We'll *all* be investigated if that happens. Have you any *idea* what could happen to Solas? What could happen to…'

'Prudence! Focus! They'll get in if your defences are down.' Delores could hear the panic in her own voice now. She reached for Prudence's shoulder, but she swerved.

'They haven't tried to read me for days,' she said. 'It upsets them too much to see Maud and she's pretty much all I think about. The stuff I do, with the food and the books, it stops me thinking about her. Even if it's only for a few minutes it feels worth it. Bet you think I'm a horrible person. I *know* I'm horrible. I should have listened to her, warned her. She got her skills really young; she was way too trusting. She trusted those children, those ghosts. I should have protected her.'

Delores knelt down beside Prudence. It was clear to her that Prudence was in pain. It explained a lot about her: not everything – and it wasn't an excuse – but Delores could relate.

'Is this the bit where we hug and become friends?' she asked.

Prudence took a neatly folded tissue from her pinafore pocket. 'No, *Delores*, it isn't. Like I said, I'm a horrible person. You know it; I know it. Let's keep it like that.' Prudence wiped her nose. 'I don't even like you, but maybe I can work with you. I don't want Maud to suffer any more, I owe her that, and I want Gabriel back. He understands me in a way you never will. Like a brother, only better. So no, not friends, not like me and him, not ever.'

'I guess I'll have to settle for allies then,' said Delores. 'I don't think we've got long before the Uncles check on him. The frost and the webs can't have been here before, or they'd have noticed.' Delores felt sick at the thought that Angel might come back, take what she wanted from Gabriel, use him to punish her.

'I can distract Oddvar,' said Prudence. 'Fingers crossed Solas has been "shifting"; he always sleeps for hours afterwards. You get all the stuff together that you've got so far, and we can take a look before we head out.'

'Stuff? What do you mean *stuff*?'

Prudence stood up, smoothed her pinafore yet again, and tucked her hair behind her ears. 'I didn't expect to have to do all the work. I saw what she was after. The book's part of it, the thing she wants. It's hers, isn't it? They need a connection to the world, a possession. It anchors her here. Don't you listen to any of the lessons? I'm guessing Maud's the thing she needs, or her ghost at least. Not sure why yet.' She tutted at the puzzled look on Delores' face. 'Ughh. What now?'

'I'm not sure Maud is completely ... dead.'

'What do you mean? I saw her, in your head, the way she looked, the way she was. Why would you even *say* that?'

Delores could see the levels of anxiety rising in Prudence's face and her hand was tapping against her leg. 'Prudence, you have to stop. Breathe. Not the best time to freak out!'

Prudence placed her hands flat against her legs and pressed hard, quashing the tapping and breathing away the panic.

'If she's not completely ... dead, can she be saved?'

'Honestly?' said Delores. 'I don't know but I'll try anything. It might be crossing that boundary Oddvar's so keen on. We can't tell them. Will you please help me?'

For the first time since they met, Prudence looked unsure. 'What about Gabriel? He looks like he's had his life-force snatched right out of him. Is that what she's doing? Is she ... feeding off us?'

Delores felt sick. Prudence had nailed it.

'That's exactly what she's doing. I saw her. She told me she'd attacked Gabriel. She was stronger than she was before; her voice was almost human again. She was still dragging death around with her, but she was changing, evolving.' It was Delores' turn for self-doubt as she thought back to Angel's manifestation in the gardens. What if she wasn't strong enough to stop her? *More than a dolls' tea party* her sister had said when the Bòcan attacked her back home, and this couldn't be farther from the companions she'd had as a child. Angel Barguest was in a whole other league.

'Maybe you were right to start with,' she said. 'Maybe we should risk telling the Uncles ... get the proper authorities...'

'No! You've no idea what we'd be risking.'

Delores rubbed her hands through her hair. 'It might help if I had all the facts?'

'You know what you need to. We'll have to take the fight to her. If we do it here, winning could turn out to be as bad as losing, for me as well as for you.' Prudence checked her wrists and pulled her cuffs down. She caught Delores looking. 'None of your business. Why didn't this Angel person, thing, just finish Gabriel off?'

'Taking her time with her food? Except it's our

paranormal-ness she's feeding off. Maybe she needs a steady supply.'

Prudence groaned. 'Paranormal-*ness*? Things are bad enough without you pulling made-up words out of the hat. And what's Bartleby got to do with it all? I kept seeing him when I was roaming around that wasteland you call a brain. He was creeping about in your psychic tumbleweed. You put Bartleby in danger, and I swear...'

Delores reached inside her pocket. 'It could be this.' She held the chess piece out to Prudence. Prudence took it and held it up to the light before passing it back to Delores. 'No idea what that's got to do with anything,' she said. 'I guess we need to talk to him.'

Prudence took a last look at Gabriel, then shoved past Delores, knocking her shoulder hard in her customary fashion. It was a lot less awkward than her crying, so Delores took it as Prudence's way of agreeing to help.

'We'll sort this out, Gabriel,' whispered Delores. 'And if Angel comes back, don't listen to her, don't go with her.'

Delores noticed Cook's latest treat for Gabriel on his bedside table. A nectarine polished to a shine on one side, blackened and wilting on the side nearest his bed. Next to the nectarine was a small fruit knife, similar to Oddvar's. The knife would be no protection against Angel, but Delores knew how she could put it to good use.

Outside Gabriel's door, she crouched down and carved a shape into the wooden floor. An open loop that crossed at one end, each line curling back on itself. The same protection that her mother had left outside their own cottage door: a protection against any Bòcan, a troll cross. Her sister had been right, it might keep them out, but they would still be waiting. Angel would still be waiting. As she scratched the final curl, she felt Prudence standing over her.

'You'll need a charm to seal that,' she said.

Prudence had a point. The cross on its own was never enough at home. 'I don't know any charms. I'm a Necromancer not a...'

'Witch? No, me neither. Not really.' Prudence knelt and placed her hand on the troll cross. She gestured for Delores to do the same then took a deep breath. '*This is our shield. This is our domain. We alone determine who shall pass.*' She placed her hand on top of Delores' and pressed it hard into the scratched surface.

We alone determine who shall pass.

Oddvar's lessons summed up in one simple charm.

Delores felt a warm vibration spreading through her hand to the floor. She was drawn in by the

179

sensation, as if her whole body was sinking through the lines of the troll cross. When she felt on the brink of losing herself, she snatched her hand away. 'I hope that isn't one of your illusions.'

Prudence looked mildly offended. 'I guess we're about to find out.'

As Delores followed Prudence down the stairs, her bag slung over her shoulder, a silent dark figure moved out from the shadows. Solas. He paused outside Gabriel's door, tilting his head, ruffling his feathers. He scratched at the lines of the freshly carved protection, then with two clicks of his ebony beak, moved back into the dark.

16

Prudence went ahead of Delores, and when they reached the ground floor, Oddvar was sitting in his usual place, studying one of his favourite books.

'Ahh, ladies. How nice to see you both occupying the same space with so little consequence. Getting along together at last?'

'Not exactly,' said Prudence. She waved her hand behind her back, signalling Delores to go through to the shop. Delores took her coat from the hook and left them to it.

A few minutes later, she was joined by Prudence, silently fastening the gold buttons on a long scarlet coat. It fitted her perfectly and complimented her sleek hair. The contrast of the dark stitching against the red emphasised its exquisite tailoring. Delores looked at the cuffs of her own navy pea coat. They were scuffed to a dull grey on the edges and one of the buttons was missing, but she'd bought it with her mum a couple of years before, so she would always love it. She caught Prudence staring at the shabby cuffs, one eyebrow raised, and responded with an equally arched eyebrow.

Prudence let slip a smile. 'Each to their own.'

'For sure,' said Delores, smiling back. 'What did you tell Oddvar?'

'That Gabriel was fine, and he'd asked to be allowed to sleep through dinner. I *suggested* that the customers were few and far between, so we were going to head to Surgeons' Hall for an early evening lecture.'

'And he swallowed it? Me and you going somewhere together?'

'He was so engrossed in his book that he was quite open to … *suggestion* … but you never know with Oddvar so can we just get on with it?'

They woke Bartleby from his late afternoon nap. He was grumpy at being disturbed and wouldn't speak to them until Delores dashed across to Esme's shop for some sherbet straws.

The girls watched as he bit the top off one, stuck his long pointed tongue out as far as it would go and then sprinkled the sherbet along it. His tongue shot back in and he smacked it against the roof of his mouth.

Prudence took the last three straws from Delores. 'You can have these later,' she said. 'We need a chat first, Monsieur Bartleby.'

Delores took the chess piece out of her pocket. 'You said this was for protection. Against Angel. Do you know who she is?'

Bartleby shook his head. '*Who*? Non. *What*? Oui. C'est une démone.'

Delores rested back on the floor, cross-legged. 'She's not a demon for heaven's sake. Why does everyone keep saying that? She's a Bòcan. I don't raise demons from … wherever it is they come from.'

Prudence tutted. 'Maybe he's speaking figuratively. Like, she's a really evil Bòcan, a demonic presence or something.'

Bartleby nodded frantically. 'Oui, yes, yes, c'est un mauvais esprit, *evil*.' He pointed at the chess piece. 'Le petit soldat? He is protection for you, ma petite coccinelle. La démone, she wants you. She wants sweet Maud. She wants…' Bartleby reached up for another sherbet straw '…all of you. Et les suivants.'

Prudence caught the confusion on Delores' face. 'Les suivants,' she said. 'The next ones. It's French.'

'I know it's French,' snapped Delores. She also knew from what Bartleby said that Angel was never going to stop. Maud wouldn't be enough. None of them would.

'How does the chess piece work, Bartleby?' she asked.

Bartleby smacked his tongue against the roof of his mouth again, narrowed his eyes and shuddered a little. 'Oh, c'était aigre!' he chuckled. 'Sour!' He stuck his tongue back out, blue now from the sherbet. He placed his finger on the shield the chess piece was holding, rubbing it gently over the engraving. 'A spell from the Old North. Shield of terror. Hold it in front of you and your enemy will see what they most fear, *dragons maléfiques*.'

Prudence turned to Delores. 'Evil dragons in case you didn't follow.'

Delores stayed calm, but her patience with Prudence was hanging by its very last thread. 'I worked it out,' she said. 'I'm not a total idiot. Dragons though, Bartleby? Really?' She smiled and touched his shoulder.

Prudence tutted. Again.

'What now?' sighed Delores.

'You're an annoyingly literal thinker. What kind of Paranormal is so literal? Maybe it's something that scares you, not an *actual* dragon. And by you, I mean whoever's attacking you.'

Delores was sceptical. 'Whoever? You mean, like, Angel? Come on...'

'Use your *métapsychique*. Easy!' said Bartleby,

184

with a shrug so high it ended around his ears. He held his palms out, waiting for a response.

'Meta what? Oh, that. Signals,' said Delores, jumping in before Prudence had yet another chance to correct her.

Bartleby grumbled at Delores' lack of faith and reached up for the rest of the straws. Delores put the chess piece back in her pocket and gestured to Prudence to hand them over. Prudence stroked the top of his head, thanking him softly, reassuring him that everything had made sense, and he should rest. Until she caught Delores watching her.

'What? I'm not a complete monster,' she said. 'I'll get a couple of books from the back that might be useful. I know what I'm looking for. You'd have no chance, pea brain.'

Delores sat with Bartleby while he ate his reward. He finished the last straw and gave a magnificent, gravelly belch. Delores tapped his back and covered him with his blanket. By the time Prudence returned, he was snoring.

Prudence was carrying Oddvar's most precious book: the one bound in leather with silver clasps; the one they were never allowed to touch.

'How did you get that?' Delores ran her hand over the cover.

Prudence flushed slightly. 'Oddvar was reading it and he thinks he still is. It won't last for long, especially when I'm not concentrating on just that one thing. He'll be furious when he realises what I've done, so we'd better get on with it.'

Delores could barely stifle a giggle. 'Wow, Prudence.'

'Shut up. He'll know straight away it was me so this better be worth it. There's a book over there on Edinburgh hauntings as well, some Psychic Investigation Unit wrote it a couple of years ago. Oddvar promised to stock it in exchange for keeping a couple of secrets they'd stumbled across. It might have your "lady" in there.'

'Sure, why not. I'll get the shiny new book while you get to handle the fabulous and infinitely more interesting one. Typical.'

'They don't call me Prudence for nothing.'

When Delores returned to the counter, Prudence was already deep in thought. Her hand was hovering a couple of centimetres above a page about a third of the way through the book.

'*Noli me tangere*, don't touch,' whispered Delores.

'Glad you managed to learn that much at least. The cover's fine, it's just the pages you have to watch out for. Probably scare tactics to limit who reads it, but I'm not taking any chances.' Prudence moved her hand to the side and the page turned.

'Impressive,' said Delores.

'Not really, and every time I do it, I lose a bit more of my grip on Oddvar so shut up and listen. I can't follow all of it. Some of it's in old French, some German and a smattering of Latin to complicate things, but basically for such a strong apparition, there has to be a connecting object. I was right about that much. How did you get her book?'

'I kind of liberated it.'

'Liberated? You mean you stole it?'

Delores nodded. 'I'd have taken it back eventually. Bet they didn't even miss it.'

Prudence stared at her.

'Oh, for heaven's sake, Prudence, blink already. What is it with you?' Delores breathed a sigh of relief when the blink finally came.

Prudence averted her gaze. 'What's important,' she said, 'is that you brought the book out into the open. It was safe where it was. If she needs one of her earthly possessions to still exist in this life so she can claw her way back, the book makes her vulnerable. It's a physical connection we can break and I'm guessing that's why she's so desperate to get it away from you. She'll be assuming you haven't figured it out yet. Which isn't surprising.'

Delores rolled her eyes at yet another dig. 'I'd have got there eventually. I'm sure there's stuff *you* don't know.'

'Of course you are,' snorted Prudence. 'You find anything?'

'Nothing I didn't already know about Angel. She murdered her children, you know.'

Prudence kept reading. 'I didn't. Anything about location? Her death?'

'She was meant to hang but she escaped from Calton jail, something about a giant … raven. You don't think…?'

Prudence stayed tight lipped. She did the slow blinking thing again. 'Just get on with the story. Thinking doesn't work well for you.'

'Don't you ever give up? Anyway, she hid in the vaults under South Bridge; that's where she died. There is a picture of her though, and one of the painting.' Delores held the book under Prudence's nose. Prudence pulled her head away in disgust.

'I saw her in your head, thanks.'

'Well, you saw the painting as well then. Those kids are creepy as. There's one particular area of the vaults where the psychics picked up a lot of activity. Said they all felt a *strong malevolent presence*. Lots of vowing never to go back there.'

There was a noise from the back room. Both girls stood in rigid silence as they looked towards the door. The sound of a chair scraping against stone. Then nothing. When Delores looked at Prudence, she saw beads of sweat on her forehead. Prudence closed her eyes and Delores saw the tell-tale sign of a tiny bit of her tongue protruding between her teeth. Another scraping of chair legs.

'He's back at the table, but I can't hold him much longer. Which part of the vaults?'

'Says most activity's around the old wine vaults and an area called the *occult chamber* on account of some rumours of torture and sacrifice, not to mention the rather lovely sounding Damnation Alley. Based on that, I'm really hoping it's the wine vault.' The girls exchanged a glance.

'Me too,' said Prudence. She looked over her shoulder. 'He's slipping out of the illusion. He's starting to probe around with his own thoughts. I am in *so* much trouble. What's the plan?'

'Uhmm…'

'Oh, come on, don't tell me you don't have a plan by now.'

Delores thought for a moment. 'Not exactly, but I'm hoping if we can pin her down and destroy the link, we might get rid of her. You'll need to try to reach out to

Gabriel, so we know if she's loosening her grip on him.'

'Or tightening it.'

'Exactly. From what you've said, the book should help draw her out. I can see why she'd be desperate to have it.'

Prudence was looking more frantic with each sound from the back room. 'Why don't we just take the book somewhere and burn it?'

'Angel took Maud that day. Whatever happens, we need to find Maud's body. We need to end this torture for Maud's sake.'

Prudence waved her hand over the pages, flipping them back to the start. She picked up a pen from the counter and used it to lever the book closed. She took great care to make no contact with its contents then placed her hand gently on the cover. 'And what's to stop that monster grabbing her book *and* what's left of Maud?'

Delores hoped that the ideas taking shape in her head were some kind of instinct, but it felt worryingly like she was making it up as she went along. 'A troll cross,' she blurted. 'Like with Gabriel. I can protect Maud and the book. She won't be able to cross its boundary. We draw her out, destroy the book and find Maud's body. Gabriel should be safe, and Maud – we'll just have to hope.'

Prudence looked far from convinced. 'If you're

wrong and what you do attracts a Gathering, you won't be the only one caught up in it.'

'And if we do nothing, Maud could be lost and scared forever.'

The door to the back room rattled again.

Prudence nodded. 'Fine, but we have to go. Have you got everything? The book, the chess piece, the calling card. We just need…'

'Maud. We need Maud. Only way to convince Angel we're really going along with it.'

'Can you call her? Convince her to come?'

Delores looked over to the corner where Maud had stood waiting for Gabriel to see her. 'She's here,' she whispered.

Delores held out her hand. 'Don't be scared, Maud, please. We'll protect you; I promise.'

Maud hesitated.

'Can you hold Oddvar a bit longer?' Delores asked, but Prudence was distracted, staring into the space where she believed Maud might be.

'Prudence, *can* you?'

'No,' said Prudence, 'but I can block the door.'

Prudence ran over to the freestanding table, heavy with books, and started to push. As the table legs screeched against the stone floor, books tumbled from the sides, leaving numerous bestsellers and 3 for 2s in its wake.

There was a complaining sound unsuitable for polite company as Bartleby turned over in his basket. He peeped over the edge.

'Maud. Mon Dieu!' His chin trembled and he settled back again, cross-legged. His head was bowed beneath his arms and he was weeping.

Prudence wedged the table up against the door as the handle turned.

'Prudence my dear,' said a raspy voice from the other side of the door. 'Let me out now and we shall consider todays actions without anger.' But there was an edge of anger in Oddvar's voice that neither of them had heard before. Prudence turned to Delores and signalled her to hurry up.

'Maud,' said Delores, 'take my hand. Please.'

Prudence put her hand on Delores' shoulder to steady herself. Her breaths were shallow and fast.

'You OK?' asked Delores.

'No, of course I'm not OK. How could I possibly be OK?' Prudence's voice was thick with tears. 'I'm not sure I see her. Maud, I'm so…'

'You might have to look slightly to the side, catch her in the edge of your vision.'

'I can't…'

'Remember what I said Prudence, you're the queen of all things paranormal. Just try and tune in to her.'

There was a pause of a couple of seconds, and then a tiny, almost imperceptible gasp. 'I think I see her but only faint, a smudge of yellow, not much else.'

Maud stepped forward into the light. Delores could see Maud in detail, but those details were thinner, less substantial now. Angel was winning. Time was running out.

When Delores turned back to Prudence, she could tell she was still struggling, looking around the edges of Maud, rubbing her eyes as if it might help. Prudence held out her hand, trying to find Maud in the space in front of her but soon dropped her arm to her side.

'I'm sorry,' said Delores. 'I really thought…'

'Don't. Just don't.'

Prudence couldn't see Maud reaching out for her, so Delores took her hand instead. Maud's lips were blue, and she was almost expressionless. Delores could hear a whisper and could see Maud trying to articulate something. She tuned in to the thin metallic sound of Maud's voice.

I'm in the dark. Help me. Please.

'We will find you, Maud, I promise.' Delores couldn't hold back the tears any longer.

17

Prudence locked the shop door behind them and slipped the key into her pocket. The sun was setting and the air was cold and damp. 'They'll get that lock open pretty quick,' she said, 'but we'll get a bit of a head start. Oddvar won't be keen on following us while it's still light, but you know how quickly it gets dark here.'

Esme was closing up the sweet shop. She waved at Delores and Prudence, then stopped as she looked past them, over their shoulders. She narrowed her eyes as if to check what she was seeing and then her face brightened. Her waving accelerated into some kind of half-maddened flapping and she was ignoring the girls as much as they were pretending to ignore her.

'She's one hundred per cent weird,' said Delores, as they walked on. 'She was going on about Solas as if she knew him. It's not likely, is it? I mean, he wouldn't … you know.'

'Shapeshift?' Prudence shivered as she looked back towards the Tolbooth. 'He most definitely would, and if Oddvar isn't keen on coming out, it makes sense to send someone who might be. They're not that bad, you know. They're trying to protect us.'

'Feels like they protect some more than others,' muttered Delores.

Prudence didn't react; she was too busy glancing over her shoulder as they headed up the hill towards South Bridge, the spectre of Maud trotting along beside them.

Delores was sure they were being followed but only caught glimpses of dark shadows as they slipped into the many closes and wynds that joined the High Street to more discreet areas of the Old Town. The Bòcan outside the tavern was back and reached out to her as she passed, catching the edge of her coat. It was a vague movement, half-hearted and short-lived, but her signals were definitely raised. The others Delores saw roaming the High Street barely paid them any attention, just a ripple of recognition, then a settling disinterest, but there was one figure, in particular, that seemed to be following at a distance. It was taller than any adult she knew, male by the way it moved and dark as pitch. A long flowing coat billowed out behind it in the growing Edinburgh wind. 'Solas,' she whispered, and grabbed Prudence's arm to urge her forward.

Prudence extricated herself from Delores' grip as they reached the corner of Blair Street, home of the infamous vaults. A tour group was approaching from the opposite direction and Prudence held up her hand, calling the group to a halt. The tour leader was a pale girl with bright pink hair, plaited neatly into two chunky braids. Her face was liberally sprinkled with piercings and the brightly coloured tattoos that peeped out from under her collar reminded Delores of the figures on Gabriel's tarot cards. She wore a black cape lined with red and Doc Martens that looked as if they'd had several not very careful owners. A badge on her cape announced her as Katy Starr. Delores liked her instantly and cringed at what she knew was about to happen.

'Miss Starr,' said Prudence, 'we have tickets. We're late but you *really* don't mind. You won't even notice us at the back.' Katy Starr looked puzzled and referred to a checklist pinned to her clipboard. Delores noticed the familiar smirk on Prudence's face and the point of her tongue between her teeth. It only took a few moments for Katy Starr's quizzical expression to relax into a semi-vacant smile as she ushered the whole group into Blair Street.

'Ironic really, isn't it,' whispered Prudence to Delores. 'So completely focused on this tour that they're missing the very thing they're looking for, right next to them.' Prudence let out a half-sigh, half-laugh but her face was run through with disappointment at her own inability to see it too.

Maud moved behind Delores, made self-conscious by Prudence's remark. 'Don't worry,' said Delores. 'They can't see you, I'm sure of it.'

When they reached the door to the vaults, Katy gathered the group in front of her, doing a quick body count and shaking her head. She shrugged and went back to her rehearsed script.

Prudence and Delores shuffled around impatiently at the back, trying to keep warm. Delores' ears pricked up when Katy neared the end of her current monologue, '…later, the vaults were home to a variety of ne'er-do-wells, gamblers, illegal whiskey distillers – even body snatchers stored corpses here. Who knows … even the notorious Burke and Hare? Not that that was ever proved.' She coughed the last sentence into her hand. 'OK then, in we go!'

Katy and her tour group shuffled inside. Prudence propped open the door, but Delores hung back.

'Something wrong?' Prudence asked.

'What do *you* think?' Delores looked past Prudence into the tourist entrance, seeing if there was anything other than leaflets and candles.

Prudence shrugged. 'What?'

'I avoid these kinds of places.'

'Surely it's *exactly* your kind of place.'

'You think? It could be full of them. You heard what the tour guide said. What if I get … over-run? They're not all like Maud. Some of them grab at me, try to get me to drag them back through. That's how I ended up with the Uncles in the first place.'

Prudence's vague attempts at patience were also coming to an end. 'We live next to a graveyard for heaven's sake. How bad can it be?'

'A graveyard, in case you haven't noticed, that I *never* go in.'

'No. Me neither.'

Prudence looked past Delores, trying to see Maud but turned away at the sound of Katy Starr's voice further inside the building. 'Close the door please,' she shouted. 'The door has to be closed before the tour of the vaults begins. Can't be letting any of our ghosts out onto the street, now, can we?' There was a smattering of nervous laughter from the tour group.

Delores rolled her eyes and then grabbed

Prudence's arm. 'Hundreds of people used to live down there, in the vaults. A lot of them probably good honest people, but a lot of bad ones too. Body snatchers, she said. There could be a lot of very unhappy over-stayers down there.'

Prudence firmly removed Delores' hand from her arm. 'Exactly. The key word is 'lived'. They didn't all die down there, stupid. Isn't that how it works?'

'No, not always. Some showed up in my house when I was little, some out on the causeway and on the beach. It must depend on what happened, what's drawing them back.' Delores felt an overwhelming desire to run out onto the street. As she turned to leave, Prudence grabbed her shoulder, spinning her slightly. 'Use what you've learned,' said Prudence. 'Shut them out, like you did with me, like you did with Oddvar. Same principal: reject the uninvited.' Delores tried to pull away again, but Prudence wasn't giving up. 'We have to help Maud and we have to get rid of Angel, preferably before she kills Gabriel. We don't know for sure that Angel can't pass that troll cross – or how long the charm will last. Like you pointed out, neither of us are *actual* witches.'

'But you said…'

'I *said* I guessed we'd find out.'

Prudence looked around her, checking no one was

listening and hoping if they were, the conversation would be dismissed as ridiculous. 'Get a grip of yourself; you see these things all of the time.'

Delores pulled herself free. 'Easy for you to say; *you* freaked out and you couldn't even *see* Maud.'

Delores wished she could take those last words back. As Prudence's hands slipped from Delores' shoulders, she looked as if she's been slapped. She turned and walked deeper into the building, followed by Maud. Maud looked back and Delores felt stabbed by the look she gave her.

'Prudence, Maud, wait. I'm sorry.'

Delores gave one last look out onto the street and walked inside. She was vaguely aware of the door slowly closing, the creaking of the springs, and how the door seemed to pause slightly, allowing for a latecomer, but Delores was too concerned with what might lie in front of her to worry about who had come in behind.

Once they were past the tourist reception, the group descended a spiral stone staircase, each step painted with a yellow strip for safety. Delores wished uneven steps were the only thing she had to worry about. The walls were whitewashed and lined with metal sconces, each with a lit candle that flickered and projected the shadows of the tour group onto the wall. Occasionally Maud cast her own shadow. Delores saw Prudence reach out for it at one point and then catch herself from falling.

As they went deeper into the vaults, the temperature dropped, and the clinging dampness rose. Three unsubstantial Bòcain, vague outlines, little more than visual echoes, passed them on the stairs. They moved upwards and reached their arms towards the door at the top. Prudence shuddered and looked round at Delores for an explanation, some reassurance. Prudence sensed them passing by her but couldn't see them. Delores gave her a weak smile and mouthed *It's fine*. The Bòcain moved by without trying to make any contact and Delores felt no threat from them. These minor apparitions seemed unaware of her, disinterested, more like simple ghosts than true Bòcain.

When they finally reached the lower level of the vaults, the tour group seemed to synchronise their movements and reach at once for the hand torches they were carrying in various bags and pockets.

'Guess we should have thought of that,' whispered Delores, then watched as Prudence convinced an American family that they only needed two torches, not four, and how kind of them to offer.

The air smelled of brick dust, as if the whole

place had been obsessively swept, scattering dust particles into the air, only for them to settle again. As Delores looked around, she sensed a movement in the shadows. She couldn't pick out any outlines, any individual figures, but there was a kind of heaving, a dark gossamer. The dragging sensation grew in her stomach and legs, and the fine hairs on her arms and neck were rigid. She could see Prudence squirming and then smoothing her coat as if she could iron the disturbance out. Delores could tell by the look on her face that she was having little success.

The tour group giggled, messed around with phone cameras and held torches under their chins as they took pictures and made 'spooky' noises. Katy Starr called them forward and they headed into a series of passages.

The dragging feeling dug in deeper, and Delores felt like she was being pulled through water by an invisible current, like the air was being stolen from her lungs, gasp by gasp. Her thoughts flashed back to the gallery. *Don't pass out. Whatever you do, don't pass out*, she told herself. A flickering at the edge of her vision drew her eye to a chamber off to one side. There stood the grey figure of a young boy, a Bòcan standing amongst a pile of small toys and fake flowers, superstitious offerings from previous tours. She wondered what a child who'd probably been dead for hundreds of years made of a plastic bus or an action figure.

Delores could tell the Bòcan was watching her, and she could make out his ragged clothes, his bare feet. She looked away slightly to put him back at the edge of her vision, trying to gather more detail. His face was passive at first, his dark eyes sad like Maud's, but there was a sudden change, as if someone had flicked a switch. He stood taller and grew more solid, the dull brown of his clothes showed through their former greyness and some facial features became visible: a sharp nose, a jutting jaw. He stepped forward, reaching out his hand as he grabbed at the space in front of him, trying to reach Delores.

Delores closed her eyes. 'Reject the uninvited. Reject the uninvited,' she whispered, as she visualised the boy being pushed back up against the wall, and then slowly through it. She felt a light resistance, a buzzing in her head, an attempt at clouding her thoughts. She thought of the silver ball, of playing with Maud. She pushed again. When she opened her eyes, he was gone. She staggered forward a step and her stomach dropped, like when you miss your footing on a stair, or that moment you leave the top of a roller coaster. The adrenaline buzz from her first success masked what the boy had taken with him, made her less aware of a little pocket of exhaustion building deep inside her.

Delores caught up with Prudence and Maud at the back of the tour as they explored the tunnels, and as the tourists diverted into chambers, swallowing the stories that Katy Starr fed them whole.

Maud was gripping the back of Prudence's coat and Prudence reached behind her from time to time, feeling for something that might or might not be there. Delores' jaw tightened. She knew she had no claim over Maud, no right to feel jealous of the heart-felt connection between Maud and Prudence, but she could barely control it. When Maud stopped abruptly and stood rigid in the middle of the tunnel, Delores snapped out of it. Maud tugged on Prudence's coat and Prudence swatted the space behind her, as if her coat was caught on something. Maud let go and turned to face Delores. She pointed at a wooden door on Delores' left.

The door had been pale blue once, but the paint had almost peeled away. A rusted lock hung loose from one nail and the door had a yellow and black sign stuck to it:

Danger of falling masonry. Keep out.

At first glance there was nothing significant

about the door, but Maud's pointing made Delores look closer. She shone her torch around the edges but only saw brief glimpses of the darkness beyond through the gaps in the rotting wood and the tangle of cobwebs that attempted to block any cracks. As her gaze drifted down, she saw white crystals of ice across the bottom edge of the door. She knelt down and in the torchlight she could see her breath appearing on the air as thick hoar frost crept slowly out from the room beyond. Her hand trembled as she reached out to touch the crystals, expecting the same bone-aching cold that she'd felt when Angel touched her. But when Delores' fingers made contact with the ice, the light from her torch fizzed and flickered out.

'What is it?' asked Prudence. Delores nodded towards the door and Prudence put the flat of her palm up against it and then her cheek. She closed her eyes, as if she was listening for something. She shrugged and shook her head at Delores.

'I feel kind of uncomfortable, in my stomach,' she said, 'but that's it.' Prudence turned away from the door and jumped as a pale face loomed out of the darkness of the tunnel. Its pallid features were exaggerated by the light from Prudence's torch and Delores cringed as the lumbering figure of Katy Starr pushed its way through Maud.

'Don't leave the group,' said Katy. 'It can be dangerous and I'm responsible for getting you out of here alive!'

Prudence groaned. 'Hilarious. You haven't seen us, Katy Starr.'

Katy peered at them, puzzled.

'Check your sheet,' said Prudence. 'Here, use my torch. All of your guests are accounted for and probably not long before they all die of boredom, so off you trot.'

Katy's face took on the blank appearance of a sleepwalker. She nodded, turned, and headed back along the tunnel, taking Prudence's torch with her, still checking her list.

'Damn, she's got my torch,' said Prudence, and went to go after her.

'Don't bother,' said Delores. 'Mine died the minute I touched the door.'

'You think this is the place?'

Delores nodded and looked up at the candle in the sconce on the wall. 'We'll take this.' She reached up to take hold of the lit candle but pulled her hand back sharply as she made contact with the hot wax. Prudence tutted, took a pair of gloves from her pocket and took the candle down herself.

'Of course you have gloves,' sighed Delores.

'Shall we?' asked Prudence, nodding towards the door.

Delores pressed both hands firmly against the door. Nothing. She pushed harder and then banged against it with her hip. No movement. Not even the hard kick that followed shifted it. She rested her forehead against the door in frustration, but quickly stepped back as the familiar gnawing cold seeped through her skin and deep into her skull.

'Try knocking?' Prudence suggested. 'Maybe she needs to let us in, invite us over the threshold?' She shuddered and pulled her arms tight around her body as Maud slipped behind her again, peeping out from the edge of her coat.

'We're not vampires for heaven's sake,' muttered Delores.

'I don't know. You think of something then, genius.'

'Fine. I'll try knocking.'

Delores tapped three times on the door and listened for a response. Silence. She knocked harder but all she got was the sensation of the miserable cold gnawing through her knuckles again.

She let her bag slip from her shoulder. The book was weighing even heavier – another sign, she guessed, that they were in the right place. She took the book out, hoping it would give her a clue or else stir something up on the other side of the door. When nothing happened, she opened it to the title page and ran her hand over the inscription. She focused on the words, the curl of the letters but was interrupted by the sound of footsteps in the corridor behind them. She glanced over her shoulder, but all she could see was the white walls fading quickly into darkness. Delores paused for a moment, trying to figure out if the footsteps were moving towards them. They stopped.

'Did you hear that?'

'I did. We'd better get on with it.' Prudence held the candle closer to the book.

Delores turned back to the inscription and muttered the words under her breath, *To my darkest Angel, my Lady of the tower.* She felt the familiar prickling in her fingers and the frost inched a little further out across the floor, edging up the sides of her boots. Something fluttered from between the pages and landed at her feet. Angel's calling card.

'Worth a try,' they both said at the same time. Prudence allowed herself the most meagre smile, contained neatly at the left corner of her mouth.

'You scared?' asked Delores. Prudence looked straight at her, and Delores was sure she was going to deny it.

'Very,' said Prudence.

'Me too,' whispered Delores.

There was a noise in the corridor behind them, footsteps again, then a flicker of a shadow across the wall. 'Someone's coming. We need to hurry.'

Prudence nodded. 'Wrong direction for it to be Katy Starr.'

'Who then?'

'I … it doesn't matter, does it? Let's just get in there.'

Delores used the edge of her boot to clear some of the ice from the bottom of the door. She bent down and slipped the card underneath. Maud reached out for Delores' hand and tightened her grip as the lock clicked and the door opened, just a few centimetres but enough for a sigh of cold air to escape.

Delores took the book and checked her pocket for Bartleby's lucky chess piece. Its heavy bulk was reassuring and made her long for the Tolbooth, for Bartleby, even Oddvar. It was a longing she wanted to reserve for her little cottage at Cramond, for her sister, but it refused to give way. She was angry that Angel had followed her to her new home, dared come inside, attacked Gabriel. She'd made her feel vulnerable, backfooted, but now she was on Angel's turf, and it was time to end this.

18

Delores placed the flat of her hand against the door. The ache that leached upwards towards her shoulder told her there was definitely something waiting for them and the look of terror on Maud's face squashed any final doubts that it would be Angel.

'Ready?' Delores whispered.

Prudence and Maud nodded. Delores pushed a little more firmly against the door. There was no creaking, just a soft slushy hiss as its lower edge pushed back a thickened layer of frost.

Prudence moved in tightly behind Delores and held the candle above shoulder height, casting a faint yellow glow ahead of them that soon turned to darkness again a few steps beyond. The door creaked closed behind them and the rusted, abandoned lock clicked into place.

As they stepped further inside, the air felt heavy, resistant to normal, living breaths. The walls glistened as the light moved over them, slick with ice and draped in exquisite swathes of silver spiderwebs. The frosted ground shimmered in the candlelight and was scattered with frozen, fat-bodied spiders, trapped in their final movements forever. As Delores drew in a deeper breath, she caught the familiar smell of peppermint backed with a tinge of sulphur. Maud sobbed gently by her side.

'Get behind me, Maud, and stay there whatever happens. She'll need to come through me to get to you.'

'Us. She'll need to come through us,' Prudence whispered. She reached out to Delores and they touched hands briefly, each quickly withdrawing.

They could hear a gentle humming. Delores didn't recognise the melody but it was light, distracted, and carefree. It echoed around the room, moving behind them, and then to the side, as if they were being circled. Prudence raised the candle higher to spread the light. She put her hand on Delores' shoulder and Delores could feel her trembling.

As Prudence moved the light across the room, they got the sense of a larger cavernous space, lined mainly with old brick but some parts of the walls were crumbling, with rubble at their lower edges. The light flickered, exaggerated by Prudence's shaking hand as it permeated the thick blackness of the far corner. As their eyes adjusted, they could make out a figure, kneeling with its back to them, gently rocking in time to the melody. A dark coat spread out behind the figure like a fan, the brightly coloured birds embroidered there glistening in the candlelight. Thick chestnut hair fell down its back in waves.

'Angel,' said Delores.

The humming stopped abruptly. The figure straightened, still kneeling. Delores and Prudence held their breath. A few seconds passed with no movement from Angel then there was a click as Angel cocked her head to one side, still not looking, but listening.

'Can you see her?' whispered Delores.

Prudence nodded. 'Why can I? Does that mean she's … alive?'

'No … but she must be close,' said Delores. 'Ready?'

Prudence shook her head.

'Me neither, but let's do this anyway.'

Angel turned her head to look over her shoulder. They could only see her dark, hollow eyes at first, but as she dropped her shoulder the red-lipped smile, the bone-white skin shone in the candlelight. 'How good of you to accept my invitation,' she said.

As Angel spun round, her coat swished behind her. There was an ethereal grace to the way she brought her leg round to her front and then stood with no effort. She clasped her hands in front of her. 'And you brought the illusionist. Prudence, isn't it? Would you like to try your illusions on me? Or do you keep them for the living?'

Prudence pulled down her cuffs over her wrists. 'Just for the living so far,' she said, 'but there's a first time for everything.'

Angel mimicked Prudence, tugging at her own cuffs. 'Hiding some tricks up your sleeves? Going to make yourself useful at last? You were no use to Maud.' Angel gestured behind her, and took an exaggerated step to one side, as if presenting a sideshow. In the dark corner, they could make out the yellow of Maud's coat and the outline of a small body lying on the ground.

Delores heard Prudence stifle a gasp.

Maud moved to the side of Delores to catch a glimpse of her own body, and then quickly moved back. She put her arms around Delores' waist and pressed her head into the middle of her back. Delores reached behind to comfort her, finding only air.

'Oh look, you brought the thing I need,' said

Angel. 'Little ghostly Maud, *my* Maud. Come to Angel wee Maud Kinloch.' Angel stepped forward, an even movement, not quite gliding. She had a hand outstretched looking slightly to the side of Delores, searching for her prize. As she got closer, Delores could see the gossamer thin covering of face over skull once more, life finely balanced on top of death.

'Stay back,' hissed Prudence. 'You think we're just going to give her up? To a *monster* like you?' Prudence waved the candle in front of her, warding Angel off. Delores reached to steady Prudence's arm. She shook her head at her, tried to calm her, but she could see the rage surfacing on Prudence's face.

Angel laughed as she came to a halt in the middle of the room. She placed one hand under her own chin and pouted. 'But what choice do you have, Prudence? But forgive me, yes, you do have a choice. Protect pretty-much-dead-Maud or...'

Prudence held her hand up to stop Angel's monologue. 'Pretty much dead?' She looked across at Delores and Delores gave an almost imperceptible nod.

Angel hesitated, as if to process her error. 'Mere semantics,' she said. 'Or you could save lovely, sweet Gabriel who slips ever closer to me with every second you waste. What a pure soul that boy has. His life force will be most useful, perhaps even better than Maud's. I'd hurry and make a decision if I were you, before I change my mind. *Tempus fugit!*' Angel started towards them again. 'And my book, of course. The thing I love.' She reached out to Delores. 'I think I might have the strength to take it now.'

Delores took a step back. 'Love? You only love it because it connects you to the living. That's why you want it so much. Keep it safe, close by and you get to stay.'

Angel reached out and made a snatching movement. 'Clever girl.'

Delores pulled the book behind her. 'How do we know you'll keep your side of the bargain and release Gabriel?'

'You don't, but do you want to risk gambling with the boy's life? Give it to me and give me Maud Kinloch, or the little that's left of her.' Angel leaned across, trying again to catch a glimpse of Maud. She licked her lips. 'Come to Angel, little one, and I'll eat you all up. It won't hurt a bit.'

'Release Gabriel first,' said Prudence. Her voice was cold and hard.

Angel switched her attention. 'Poor Prudence. You could so easily have saved her. Maud told you she was talking to my children, didn't she? But clever

Prudence was too busy with her books and her charts to care very much, and my children do tell so many lies about me. They told her I was coming, and *she* told *you* but still you didn't care. Isn't it a little late to decide how important Maud is to you? Give her to me or the boy dies.'

Delores saw Angel's comments strike hard at Prudence and took her chance to step in. 'Why would we swap one friend to save another? We don't even know if Gabriel's still alive, do we, Prudence?' Prudence took her cue. She closed her eyes and then Delores heard her voice inside her head. *He's there, I think. I'll keep trying.*

Angel sighed. 'Now you're just being tiresome. You Paranormals are so easy; it's like shucking oysters. Your life force already loose on the half shell. And let's not forget my anchor.' Angel reached out towards the book and gestured for Delores to hand it over.

Delores pulled it tightly to her chest. 'This life is not yours any more,' she said. 'Your time is over.'

Angel drew her hand back. 'Who gets to decide that? I have things to finish. I escaped the prison and I thought he would come to find me, but he left me here to rot.' A bitter laugh tumbled out of Angel's mouth.

'He?' asked Delores, though she had a sinking

216

feeling she knew who Angel meant. 'The raven in the jail? Was it Solas Sigurdarson?'

'It can't have been,' whispered Prudence.

'Solas. My beautiful raven,' whispered Angel. 'How could he have left me here to die?' She looked at Delores, expecting an answer.

'Erm … because you're a murdering psychopath?'

Angel looked puzzled at the description. 'I waited, roamed these tunnels, driven mad with despair. I took shelter in this room, but the door slammed shut, locked from the other side and it was here that I took my last breath. A precious release I thought. But no. I found myself trapped in a dark, unfathomable space amongst a mass of heaving souls, filthy and pulsating. I had to get back to the life I'd been cheated of.'

'Cheated?' said Delores. 'You killed your own children; you got what you deserved.'

'Your interpretation. Then Maud did something wonderful. She spoke to my children, played with their ghosts in the churchyard. When she made that connection, a corridor opened and I walked along it, straight to her. My own naughty children ran away as soon as they saw me, but Maud just stood there, mouth gaping. She cried for you, Prudence. She didn't want to come into this dark place, but I was in her mind by then and she could do nothing to save herself. She simply wandered away. I started her sweet release from this world, stole her a second time. She made me strong, but the cunning little thing gave me the slip before I'd quite finished. It's rude not to finish your plate, but quite another thing for the meal to run away.'

'It's not *release*, it's *murder*,' growled Prudence. 'Just like you murdered your own children. You're a selfish monster.'

Angel struggled to conceal her anger. 'Give her to me. Now,' she hissed. Her skin pulled itself tightly back against her skull, thinning her lips and revealing her teeth. She drew herself up to her full height and twisted her neck from side to side until her skin unstuck itself a little and her beautiful facade was back in place. There was a light snapping sound at the final twist – hardly audible but still enough of a slip to make Maud cry out.

Prudence placed the candle on the floor propped against a small stone. She smoothed her coat.

'No,' whispered Delores. 'Don't do it.' She felt Prudence scratching around in her mind, her voice distant but clear. *I have to try. Gabriel's fading. Maybe if I take her on, she won't be able to manage all of us.*

Prudence stepped forward. 'I'm not scared of you,' she said.

'Prudence don't...' begged Delores.

Prudence made eye contact with her. *The book. Do it.*

Angel beckoned Prudence forward. Prudence drew back her shoulders and shook her hair into its more usual perfect shape. She brushed down the arms of her coat and stepped between Angel and Delores.

As Prudence moved forward, Delores used the toe of her boot to draw a troll cross into the deep hoar frost that was crystallising ever thicker on the ground.

'What do you think you are going to do to me, Prudence?' asked Angel. 'Can the living trick the dead?'

'Is that what you still are?' asked Prudence. 'You've been using Maud all this time to get back to the living. How close are you? You're drawing on Gabriel too. Maybe that'll be your downfall.'

'Silly child,' laughed Angel, but there was a nervous edge to the laugh, an uncertainty that Delores hadn't heard before, but one that Prudence homed in on.

'Silly? Never. Child? Hardly. It's children you like to prey on, isn't it? Maud was easier, but Gabriel? He was still inside his body last we saw of him. Too strong for you? It's why you haven't killed us yet, isn't it? Can't manage us all at once.'

'Maybe I will kill *you*.' Angel reached out and lifted

Prudence's chin with her finger. Prudence pulled back.

Delores placed the book in the centre of the troll cross. The heaviness that she'd been feeling lifted slightly and it felt easier to breathe and move. To think.

'The charm, the charm for the troll cross, what was it?' she whispered. She placed her hand on the edge of the markings, struggling to remember, panic rising. 'Our domain something, something, our … ugh … shield… We determine who shall pass! That's it, *we determine who shall pass.*' Oddvar's lesson. In one take. The charm was cast. She hoped.

Any ease Delores felt was short lived, pushed aside by her fear for Prudence. She saw the slight flick of the head and the tucking of the hair that meant Prudence S-Dottir was about to get to work.

'Don't do it,' whispered Delores. 'Please don't.'

Prudence turned her head quickly. *It's OK. We have Maud's body, and I can feel Gabriel waking up. Together we are too much for her. I feel it: she's losing control. Destroy the book.*

Prudence turned back to Angel. 'A raven, a tower and a murderer.'

'What did you say?'

'You heard me the first time. I know the raven.'

There was a banging from the other side of the door, someone trying to get in, but Prudence held her focus on Angel. 'He helped you, didn't he? Then left you to die. Let me show you why.'

'No. You will not show me.'

The book. Now!

'He found you out,' said Prudence. 'He always does. He saw inside you, the same way I see inside people. The mask slipped and he saw what you'd done, who you really are, your dark, dark heart, your hideous soul. Your lies meant nothing then and he left you to die. I'll show you his face, how he looks when he's disappointed, how he looks when he loves you and how he looks when he hates.'

Angel leaned towards Prudence. Close enough to whisper, 'You can't know it and you can't know him, not like I do.'

'But I do know it, and I do know him,' whispered Prudence in return.

Delores could see plumes of Prudence's breath rising into the air, saw her saying something, just to Angel. An illusion? Whatever it was, it froze Angel to the spot.

Delores felt Prudence in her head again, weaker, but insistent. *The book! Do it now!*

Delores picked up the candle and held it to the

corner of the book. Her hand shook so hard that the flame flickered and danced around the corner of the front cover, not resting long enough to catch fire. The candlelight reflected from the ever-thickening frost and through it, Delores could see the rage building in Angel's face. She was not going to go lightly.

Angel grabbed Prudence, screaming for her to stop. She held her by both arms and Prudence's body went slack. Delores watched, paralysed by fear as frost began to spread down Prudence's back. Her scarlet coat turned white, and her soft hair froze into feathers of ice. Two of the spiders broke free from their icy casing and scurried up her back as the banging on the door grew louder. A voice from the other side of it screamed Prudence's name.

Angel lifted her head and tilted it as if there were a brief moment of recognition, then brought her full attention back to Prudence. She drew their faces closer together, and lifted Prudence's slack body, tilting her this way and that, watching her, the excitement growing on her face as a green-blue light emanated from Prudence. Maud's crying became pitiful, and Delores felt her grip her arm. She had to destroy the book, break the link. She had to close the corridor that she and Maud had opened. She had to save Prudence.

Delores lifted the candle, stifling a cry as the hot wax dripped onto her skin. 'Come on, come on, come on...' she begged. She looked up again and Angel was glowing. She looked fresher, younger, and Prudence lay limp in her hands. Angel pulled Prudence closer to her, ready to take the last drop of her life force. The door rattled louder. The constant shouting was more desperate – a man's voice that Delores hadn't heard before. Her hand trembled and she begged again for the book to catch light.

Then Angel caught sight of what Delores was doing. 'No!' she screamed. She let go of Prudence and Prudence's body slumped to the floor.

The corner of the book smouldered and an acrid smell of burning drifted across the room. Angel lunged at Delores, but Delores and Maud stayed behind the troll cross, praying they were untouchable. Delores dropped the book into the troll cross in fright and the tiny flame grew, but as it grew, the frost around it started melting. The troll cross was disappearing. Angel knelt opposite, waiting, hungry. The drumming on the door went on and the shouting grew more desperate. 'Prudence, it's me, your father. Open the door.'

The look of recognition registered on Angel's face once more. 'It can't be,' she said.

Delores knew she only had a few seconds while Angel was distracted, a few moments before the troll cross was gone. It was then she remembered the chess piece, Bartleby's gift, and Prudence's advice not to be so literal. Maybe the shield did hold a spell; maybe there was something that Angel was truly afraid of. She needed to buy some time, allow the book to burn.

Delores took the chess piece and held it in front of her. 'Step back,' she shouted at Angel. 'Step back now!'

Angel looked amused. 'What are you doing?' She peered at the chess piece in the half light and mimicked its face by chomping her teeth against her lower lip, laughing. The more Angel laughed the more enraged Delores became. 'Get away from us or the book burns.'

'Why would I give up now?' laughed Angel. 'I'm stronger thanks to the illusionist; as soon as your little enchantment has gone, I can take *everything*.'

Angel was right, as the crossed loops melted, she would be able to grab the book and Maud would be next. Delores took her anger and focused it on the little figure. Bartleby had told her to use her *métapsychique*, her psychic power. She squeezed the figure until the edge of its shield dug into the sides of her fingers. She ran the index finger of her other hand across the front of the shield and visualised the pattern there. She thought of dragons, black ones. She pictured them rising out of the smoke from the book, swirling around them, reaching for the ceiling and breathing fire. She imagined their roar, their anger at being disturbed. She pictured how she could control them, turn them towards Angel. When she heard a bone-cracking scream, Delores opened her eyes. Angel was standing, taking short steps back, still screaming.

Angel was not being confronted by dragons. She was surrounded by the dark gossamer of souls that Delores had seen further back in the vaults. Angel's own personal dragons. The long gone, the criminals, the body snatchers, the ones that were the faceless figures in the history of the vaults: condemned to be forgotten forever. The thing Angel Barguest feared most. Delores was shocked out of her focus by the horror unfolding in front of her, the horror she'd set in motion. One of the dark figures turned, reaching out a wasted arm of black smoke. The hand took form as it moved towards her, a mixture of bone and sinew, of hanging flesh.

'No!' screamed Delores. She refocused on the shield and its powerful charm. The dark figure turned back to its original purpose. Angel clawed at the figures, screaming at them to get away from her. 'Take them, not me!' she screamed. 'I will not go into the

225

dark with you! I will not be forgotten!'

The banging on the door stopped and was replaced by a noise Delores did recognise but louder than she'd ever heard it, the cronking and cawing of a raven.

Angel heard it too. She was screaming now, sobbing, as she reached towards the door. 'My love. You have come to save me.'

'He hasn't come to save *you*,' yelled Delores. 'He knows exactly who you are. *What* you are. Leave now! You are *uninvited*!'

The dark figures tugged on Angel's sleeves and on her body, but she was resisting, pulling away from them. 'Get this filth off me! How dare they! I am not them! I will not go with them!'

'Yes, you will,' yelled Delores. She flipped the edge of the book open, exposing the pages. She blew on the flame, begging the flimsy paper to catch light. As she blew, she felt dizzy. A grim, bone-deep tiredness was taking form, and with it, a fear that she might not have the strength to finish this. She thought of Maud, of Gabriel, of how brave Prudence had been. She gathered what energy she had left and rejected the uninvited. She kept the chess piece held high, its shield pointed towards Angel, making sure the dark spirits still surrounded her. Then she began to push forward using all of the psychic energy she could gather.

Angel staggered back. Just one step but it was enough to give Delores the will to keep fighting, the confidence that she could do it, that she could push this wretched Bòcan back to the other side where she belonged. Another step back, then another. Delores kept pushing from her mind, thinking of the silver ball, remembering how she'd played the game with Maud. Angel staggered further back into the darker realms of the room until she was up against the wall. Delores could see her white face, but the rest of Angel was a swirling mass of black, the dark spirits hanging from her like the cobwebs that she'd conjured in the bookshop. Angel tried to push them away, but they wrapped themselves around her as Delores held her against the wall with her psychic force. The pages of the book caught light at last. Delores fell back as the flames rose higher. She felt her energy falling and Angel lunged forward, reaching through the spirits, trying to grab for Delores, for the book, for anything. Angel screamed pure rage but one of the black hands covered her mouth. As the flames grew, Angel's white face became grey, her body insubstantial. The dark spirits cocooned her and then shattered into tiny pieces of soot, exploding into the air as the last echo of Angel Barguest shimmered around the edges, and evanesced.

19

The lock clicked and the door was pushed open. A tall figure ran in, his cape billowing behind him, seemingly unaware of Delores or the final remains of the burning book. He ran to Prudence and crouched beside her, lifting her gently in his arms. The frost had gone from her hair, and it was hanging wet over the collar of her coat. Delores kicked at the burning embers of the book and stamped on them to make sure they were out, to make sure there was no way back for Angel. Maud took her hand and they moved closer to where Prudence was lying.

'Uncle Solas,' Delores whispered. 'Prudence is your daughter, isn't she?'

Solas nodded. In the dim light from the candle, Delores could make out his slightly too-long black hair, standing in tufts. He had the same unblinking golden eyes as Prudence. 'Wasn't it obvious?' he said. 'I only wanted to protect her; that's all I ever wanted.' His eyes filled with tears and he looked back at his daughter. 'She's as cursed as I am. An outcast amongst outcasts. The Adjustment Council would lock her away if they knew. She'd spend her next few years waiting in a cell, while the Council watched her, waiting to see if she would move into her other-body. I won't let them do that to her.'

Solas lifted Prudence's limp body towards him and touched his forehead against hers. He closed his eyes and breathed in deeply, as if he was breathing in the very essence of her. On the second breath, his face darkened, and Delores thought she saw the suggestion of feathers in his hair. The outline of his cloak became less defined as he began to chant an incantation or a spell. Delores didn't know what it was, or care; she was just desperate for it to work, for Prudence to come back. She wanted nothing more in that moment than to be on the receiving end of one of Prudence's illusions or one of her barbed remarks. She tried to reach out to her with her signals, beg her to come back but all she felt was empty space. Then Prudence's shoulders lifted, as if she were taking a deep breath. Solas sagged a little and his dark hair became tipped with white.

'Wake up, Prudence,' he said. 'Come back to me.'

Prudence opened her eyes and whispered, 'Dad.'

Maud pulled Delores towards where her body was lying. Delores was scared to look at first, but in the shadows Maud's body looked peaceful, preserved in the frost that Angel had spun around it. She knelt down next to the body and placed her ear against Maud's mouth. Nothing. She waited. The other Maud, the essence of Maud, knelt down next to her. She took Delores' hand.

'Take the other hand. The body,' said Solas. 'There will be a cost to you, but it might work. You are the link in a chain. A true Necromancer. Believe it and it will be so. You have to give Maud permission. She is now but a traveller.'

Delores reached out and took the cold, still hand of Maud's body. She turned and smiled at the thinning, insubstantial part of Maud that stood next to her. 'Go back, Maud. Please. It's fine.'

Delores braced herself, ready for the deep gnawing feeling that she'd felt around Angel, but all she felt was a sense of falling. A soft, never-ending fall, a fading into darkness. She wondered if this was how dying felt and was ready to succumb when she heard a voice.

'Don't fall so far, Delores. She's home.'

When Delores opened her eyes Maud, the real Maud, was curled up beside her on the cellar floor. Her face was dirty, streaked with tears, and her lips looked dry and cracked. But it was definitely Maud. Solid, living Maud.

Solas was standing over them. Delores tried to get up. Her bones ached and her muscles quivered as she pulled herself up into a sitting position. Her shoulder and neck felt numb. Solas looked grim-faced and exhausted.

'We must get them back to the Tolbooth,' he said. 'Help is on its way.'

Delores nodded. 'What was it? What was the cost?'

The door creaked open, and a slender hooded figure walked in, bent slightly forward, hands held in an attitude of prayer. Oddvar.

'The cost, my dear, will be payable by all of us,' he said. 'News of such a psychic disturbance will reach the Adjustment Council quickly.'

'A Gathering?' whispered Delores.

Oddvar knelt down next to Maud. He lifted her with a divine tenderness and held her close to his chest. He shook as tears fell down his face. 'Our darling Maud, brought safe home to us,' he sobbed. Delores looked away.

Solas put his hand on Delores' shoulder. 'You must

be clear by now that using your full psychic energy like that, takes a little of you with it. If exhaustion hasn't hit you yet, it will soon. We should go.' Solas' voice was soft and rich with concern. Delores felt as if he were seeing her properly for the first time: an individual, worthwhile.

'I just have to do something first,' said Delores.

She went over to the wall where some of the plaster had crumbled and felt with her hand for any softer areas, any loose bricks or mortar. She tried with her nails and when they finally sank into an area about halfway up the wall, she managed to loosen a brick next to it and pull it out. She went back to where the fire had been and scooped up the remainder of the ash from the book. She placed the ashes in the cavity she'd made, taking care not to leave any behind. She rammed the brick back in to place and took a sharp-edged piece of stone from the floor. On the front of the brick, she scratched a troll cross.

'Goodbye forever, and good riddance, Angel Barguest,' she said. Delores turned to Solas and watched as he scooped Prudence up in his arms. At his full height, he was impressive. Maud was stirring but sleepy. Delores knelt next to her and Oddvar helped Maud up into a piggyback from Delores. Maud groaned sleepily but then squeezed tightly to hold on. The squeezing emphasised the cold numbness in Delores' shoulder, but she dismissed it as a consequence of the freezing temperature in the room.

Oddvar picked up the candle to light the way, along with the disintegrating calling card. He held it to the flame and watched it burn. As Solas carried Prudence out, Delores reached back and pulled the door closed behind them. The rusted lock clicked back into place.

'Did you do that, Solas? To the lock?' Delores asked.

Solas shook his head. 'Some things we simply don't know. Let's go.'

Oddvar placed the candle back in its sconce, his customary silk handkerchief wrapped neatly around his hand for protection. 'Everything in its own place,' he said.

In the light, Delores got a better look at Solas. She tried hard not to stare. His features were sharp, but she could see why Sweet-Shop-Esme was so interested in him. His clothes were as unusual as Oddvar's – and tailored to the same high, elegant standard. Even his boots were similar. No monocle. With Prudence still in his arms, Solas climbed the concrete steps as if it was nothing to him, as if her bones were filled with air. Delores huffed and puffed her way up behind him, feeling the full weight of Maud on her back. Oddvar trailed slightly as he pulled his hood up once more and hid his hands with black, silk gloves.

When they reached the exit, a new tour group was gathering, and Katy Starr was running through her script for the second time that evening. 'Excuse me, sir,' she shouted as Solas pushed past, 'you're not supposed to be there on your own. How...' Solas stopped and looked intently around the group, taking in each face. They all took on that familiar blank expression, even Katy Starr, but Delores figured she must be used to it by now.

'All you have seen are shadows. No marvels, no oddities. You will remember nothing of us,' said Solas. With that, he marched forward, with Delores and Oddvar struggling to keep up behind.

At first, the street seemed the same. It was busy with tourists heading out for an evening's entertainments, chatting loudly, spread across the pavements, holding hands. Noise and warm light spilled from bars and restaurants, and black cabs trundled back and forth over the cobbles. But as they moved through the crowds, Delores noticed something different. She was drawing attention. Not from the Normals, from the Bòcain. Even the vaguer, less formed ones turned to watch her pass, observing her closely as she headed back towards the bookstore. She put her head down and Maud held on tighter.

By the time they reached the Tolbooth, Delores was at collapsing point. The lights were out at the front, but the door was unlocked. As they went in, Bartleby looked out from beneath his blanket. When he saw Maud, he let out a tearful sob and then clasped his hand across his mouth. Delores nodded and smiled.

'Thank you, Bartleby, for everything.'

Bartleby stuck out his tongue, then grinned and went back to sleep.

Solas didn't falter, marching directly through to the warm glow of lights at the back and straight up the stairs. Delores dragged along behind him, gripped by the kind of weariness that makes you squirm and dream of a hot shower and a soft bed, but the first thing she wanted to do was to see Gabriel.

Suddenly her back felt lighter, cold, and Maud's hands dropped away from her neck. Delores tried to grab for her, thinking she'd let her fall, but there was nothing. She turned quickly, snatching at the air, frantic that it had all been a trick and Maud was gone. But Maud was being held in a pair of enormous arms, that belonged to the tallest, broadest person she'd ever seen. Maud snuggled instinctively into the elaborately patterned jumper that the person was wearing. The figure stepped quickly back into the shadows between the two rooms before Delores had chance to take in any detail, other than hiking boots, thick socks and a kilt.

'Cook?' she asked.

'Not now,' said Oddvar, as he took her arm. 'Maud is in safe hands. Let's check on Gabriel.'

Solas had rushed past Gabriel's door, taking Prudence to her own room. Delores hovered in the corridor and listened to the hushed words passing between them, a reprimand, some tears and then the comforting sounds of a raven soothing its young. It made her feel alone, made her miss her parents, but that was tightly bound up with a sense of exquisite relief to be back at the Tolbooth. It was a warm, comfortable feeling that was wholly unexpected.

A chair had been moved into Gabriel's room so that Oddvar could hold vigil, and in it sat a stranger. She was dressed in a fitted jacket, long tweed skirt and boots similar to the ones Oddvar and Solas wore. Her hair was cropped short and bleached white. She couldn't have been much older than Delores. There was an old-fashioned medical bag at her feet. She nodded a courteous greeting to Oddvar then turned her attention back to Gabriel, watching him intently.

'I should introduce you,' said Oddvar. 'Delores, this

is Doctor Ernaline Reid. She is a dear friend of mine, and a doctor with skills particular to the maladies of Paranormals. I feared Gabriel was beyond the scope of conventional medicine.'

'How very formal,' said the woman, eyes still fixed on Gabriel. 'Please, call me Ernaline.'

Oddvar wagged his finger. 'Most definitely not. Delores, you will address the doctor by her proper title at all times. How goes the patient, Doctor?'

'The tinctures are working,' she said. 'He's coming back to us. Hopefully he'll recover fully.'

Delores felt her body sag with relief. She could see from the doorway that Gabriel's eyes were closed but this time he was asleep. His breaths were even and the essence of what made him Gabriel had re-joined his body.

Oddvar cleaned his monocle with his silk handkerchief, then put it in his waistcoat pocket, giving it a gentle pat. 'Well, Delores Mackenzie,' he said, 'there is still quite a conversation to be had, is there not? But not tonight. I can assure you that Gabriel will remain safely under my watch and that of Doctor Reid. I believe Cook has everything in hand. Eat. Rest. Recover your strength. We will speak further in the morning. I expect you at breakfast. The usual hour.'

20

Delores had over-slept. It was already light, so she knew it was later than 6:30. She hadn't slept so deeply since before she came to the Tolbooth. As she came to, she felt like she was being watched. She kept her back turned, not wanting to look at the other bed.

Ughhh those wretched dolls, she thought. *They're going in the bin, the cupboard, anywhere – no matter what Gab—*

'You're awake!'

Delores flipped over. 'Maud! It's really you.' She tried to sit up, but her head was swimming and every part of her felt as if it had taken a battering.

Maud peeped at her from under a thin cotton sheet. Her blankets and quilt looked like they'd been kicked to the floor next to her, even though she was shivering. Her hair was splayed across her pillow and her face was shiny and clean, but so pale she looked almost grey in the morning light. Her eyes were blue, not dark, sad or empty, just a normal childhood blue. She lifted her arm from under the sheet and waved the lanky, tatty-headed doll at Delores. It grimaced.

'Glad to see you've got your dolls,' said Delores. 'Maybe tell them I'm your friend?'

'They're not mine,' said Maud. She dropped her croaky voice to a whisper. 'They belong to Agnes. She lives in the clock tower. She didn't like the graveyard. She lets me play with them.'

'Agnes?' Delores looked towards the clock-tower door.

'You'll see her.' It was Maud's turn to look at the clock-tower door. 'When she's not so grumpy. We're the same, me and you, aren't we?' She smiled.

'Do the Uncles know? About Agnes?' Delores felt a mild squirming feeling thinking what or who this Agnes might be. 'The dolls don't seem like they're happy things, Maud,' she said. 'I'm not sure Agnes should really be here...'

Maud put her finger to her lips. 'Shhh, Agnes said not to tell. Here...' She reached under her pillow, pulled out the tiny bird skull and handed it back to Delores. 'She says she's sorry she took it.'

Maud turned over and went back to sleep. As Delores watched the rise and fall of her shoulders, she realised she'd never considered the fact that she didn't really *know* Maud. She'd made assumptions about her. Time would tell, but she had to trust her gut instinct for now that Maud was the sweet and gentle soul that she'd always believed her to be, that the time with Angel had not left some kind of mark on her.

Delores washed and dressed as quickly and quietly as she could, but she was hampered by aching muscles, tired bones and a headache straight from hell. As she pulled a fresh shirt over her shoulders, Delores noticed something odd. The skin on her left shoulder was still numb. When she touched it, it felt cold and slightly raised. She leaned in towards the mirror over the dressing table to get a closer look. The numb area from her shoulder and up into the lower reaches of her neck was covered in a lacework of white marks, arranged in a feathered pattern. Not like bird feathers, more the feathered print of frost on a cold window, the pattern of the frost that had run up Prudence's back in the vault. The marks looked like slender scars or a white ink tattoo, beautiful, strange. She ran her fingers over them again. Maybe there was a physical cost to her skills other than tiredness, but for now, Delores thought, it suited her. She dressed and covered what could still be seen with her mother's scarf.

Delores' mouth was sandpaper dry, and her hunger was almost painful as she made her way to the dining table. Oddvar was waiting for her, along with a mug of hot chocolate and some freshly buttered toast. Delores didn't bother questioning such things any more. Cook was clearly phenomenal and for that she was grateful. She apologised for her lateness and Oddvar accepted with a gracious nod of his head.

'Have Prudence and Gabriel already eaten?' she asked. She was desperate to see them both. Prudence had turned out to be a bit of a badass and might even be kind of likeable – eventually.

'Gabriel is sleeping. Prudence and her father are getting ready to leave. Uncle Solas informed me that you are fully aware of their *unusual* family dynamic. I thought you might well have worked it out for yourself.'

Delores shook her head. 'I wondered about the feathers but there was so much else going on, I kind of shelved it.'

'The name S-Dottir? Quite the clue if you had taken the time,' said Oddvar. 'A shortening of Solasdottir, daughter of Solas. His Icelandic roots, so to say. They both leave today, however.'

Delores felt slightly annoyed with herself over the name. She'd had a brief obsession with Icelandic thrillers – it had only lasted a few months, but she'd still ploughed her way through enough names to have known better. The annoyance was short-lived as she took in the rest of what Oddvar had said. 'Leave?' she asked. 'Where are they going?'

'Prudence will stay with her mother while she recovers.'

Delores almost choked on her toast. 'Prudence has a mother?' She quickly wiped away the glob of melting butter that was hanging from her chin.

'Of course,' said Oddvar, wincing at the sight of the butter. He handed Delores a napkin. 'Their family home is on the Isle of Harris. Her mother is an old-school witch with no paranormal skills to speak of outside that particular field. Sadly, when it became apparent from the casting of feathers that Prudence may have inherited her father's shapeshifting abilities, she became quite afraid and sent the dear girl to us. It soon became clear that Prudence was special and needed protection. We have spoken of Gatherings, have we not?'

Delores nodded. 'I don't want that to happen to Prudence. She risked a lot to help Maud and Gabriel. And me.'

'Indeed, yet I do also accept that she can be rather challenging. To the main matter now, my dear.'

Delores swallowed her toast with some difficulty. She took a sip of her hot chocolate and nodded for Oddvar to continue.

'I have already received notification that superiors from a higher level of the Adjustment Council in Norway are aware of a period of most unusual paranormal activity in our city. Unfortunately, they have pinpointed the centre of said activity to the Old Town, more specifically on a direct route between here and the vaults. Representatives are on their way. There will be an investigation and they will wish to question everyone at the school, test that the acceptable bounds of paranormal activity have not been crossed. I am highly skilled in avoidance techniques, as you can imagine, but I fear that they would easily gain information from you. An investigator will not shy from reaching deep inside your mind and they care little for kindness.'

Delores blushed and put down her toast. 'Are you sending me away?'

'Yes, that is exactly what I am doing. If they see what has happened, you will be at risk. You also know too much about Uncle Solas and about Prudence. If their discoveries prompted a Gathering, all three of you could be taken. You have been treading on very thin ice and risking us all falling through alongside you.'

Delores could feel the tears welling up in her eyes. 'I'm sorry. I thought I was doing the right thing. I thought you might shut me down before I could help Maud and I couldn't stand the thought of that.'

Oddvar reached out to take her hand. Delores hesitated. She remembered his firm grip when they first met, how he'd warned her about her behaviour, how hard she had found it to trust him. When she looked up, he was smiling at her, the same kindness he'd shown when he had given her the silver ball, when he'd tried to get her to confide in him. She put her hand in his and it felt good.

'Quite so,' he said. 'We must all learn from this. I *am* sending you away, but with Prudence and Uncle Solas. You can return to the school when all is well. Your lack of control over your psychic signals brought that creature more vividly into our world, but I believe it was control of those same powers that sent her back. You have great potential, Delores Mackenzie. They can question Gabriel if they wish. There are blanks in his memory from his... What shall we call it? Possession? So, I feel it is safe to allow their inquisition.'

It was Delores' turn to wince. 'Possession?' she asked. 'More like attempted murder.'

Oddvar folded his hands on the table. 'Quite so, but

I think his lapses may only be temporary so we must waste no more time and, as I said, the investigation team is on its way.'

'What about Maud? Will they question her?'

Oddvar poured some more chocolate into Delores' mug from a silver coffee pot. She was grateful for the distraction. She couldn't stand the thought of Maud going through any more distress.

'Maud is below the age of questioning and the Adjustment Council are unaware of the precocious nature of her skills. She came to us in Cook's care and will remain so during the investigation. Cook is an extraordinarily powerful individual, so Maud is the safest of us all.'

Delores nodded. 'About Cook…'

Oddvar shook his head. 'Cook's story is long and fascinating, as is Doctor Reid's. We cannot do them justice when time is so lacking. Doctor Reid has agreed to step in for Uncle Solas in his absence, as both physician and teacher for Gabriel and Maud. I am very much hoping she will stay on after his return, and that you will get the opportunity to become properly acquainted. Which leaves only the packing, and one final question, if I may?'

Delores finished her drink and pushed her chair back, ready to leave. 'Sure. Ask away.'

Oddvar shuddered at Delores' informality but quickly regained his composure.

'It is clear you have some elements of control in place, so it may be possible for you to finish your education nearer your sister, in Norway perhaps? It could be arranged if you would be happier there.'

'Can I ask you something before I decide?' said Delores. Oddvar gestured with his hand for her to continue.

'My parents. Please tell me how to find them? I know they're not dead. I think I always knew that.'

Oddvar stood and moved around the table. He took Delores gently by the shoulders, as if to hold her up. 'My dear,' he said, 'you may never find them, and even if you do, as I already told you, you will never be allowed to see them through legal channels. The Council will not want them to corrupt you.' Delores tried to pull away, but Oddvar held fast. 'That is *their* word, not mine. In our own ways, we are all rebels here and, though I make no promises, I will help you in any way I can.' When he was sure Delores would stay standing, he let go.

She took a few moments to think. Norway would be a new start, it would mean being closer to Delilah, and her parents could be in the north, but that would mean leaving so much behind: Bartleby,

Gabriel, Maud – even Prudence. The thought of being taught by the two Uncles, of all the wonderful books in Oddvar's study was tempting. Add Doctor Reid into the mix and she could hardly resist. This was the first place she'd ever fitted in. The fit might not be perfect, but it was a start and a great place to find out more about the Gatherings, about what happened to Paranormals like her parents. She could find out how to be stronger, prepare herself to take on the Council, challenge her parents' captivity. This is where her journey could begin.

'I'll come back here if that's OK?' she said.

Oddvar nodded. 'Quite acceptable, Delores Mackenzie, really quite acceptable.'

Delores pushed her chair in. 'Thanks, Uncle Oddvar.'

'Uncle? How good it is to hear you call me that. Now go and pack before they decide to leave without you.'

Delores held her hands up. 'I'm going, I'm going.' As she turned to leave, she looked back for a moment. 'It felt good to saying it.'

Oddvar smiled and waved her away.

It didn't take Delores long to pack. Most of her stuff was still in the case under her bed. A few sniff tests proved slightly alarming, and she wondered if the witches of the Isle of Harris had laundry facilities. She also wondered at the impossibility of feeling so sad zipping up her case after such a short time at the Tolbooth. How could you miss somewhere you never wanted to be in the first place? She adjusted the silk scarf that covered the delicate white marks on her neck and shoulder and returned the bird skull to its travelling place in her pocket. She was ready.

Prudence had collected Maud earlier, so Delores bumped her case back down the stone stairs alone. Solas' space had been tidied. The bowl that had held fruit and seeds was empty, and the nest structure was gone. She assumed he would be holding his human form to travel; disappointing but she understood why. The absence of his nest was more concerning; it implied he might not return to the Tolbooth at all.

When she got to Gabriel's room, Delores parked her case in the doorway and stepped inside. Maud was cuddled up on the bed next to Gabriel, and Dr Reid was sitting in a chair next to them, Prudence standing at her shoulder. Prudence's eyes were fixed on Dr Reid's hair. Her hand wandered up to her own: tentative, quivering, sweeping it upwards. She touched the space at the nape of her neck as if she were picturing herself with the same short crop.

Total Fangirl. Might have known, thought Delores. Prudence glanced quickly at her, and Delores swore she saw Prudence S-Dottir blush.

Dr Reid waved her closer. 'It's fine; he's much better,' she said. 'He should see you before you leave.' There was a lightness to Ernaline Reid's voice, with softly lengthened *s* sounds that reminded Delores of leaves and moth wings. It made her feel calm and trusting. She perched on the edge of Gabriel's bed and took his hand.

Gabriel was as pale as Maud and his lips were dusky blue. He had dark patches under his eyes and his white-blond hair stood in regimented tufts. But he was awake. And he was very much Gabriel. His smile was back even if it did hover timidly behind his exhaustion.

'You took your time,' he croaked.

'Sorry. Bit busy vanquishing the dead.'

Gabriel looked puzzled and Delores realised she'd probably said too much. She could sense Prudence's agitation and heard a few hissing words inside her head about the coming inquisition. This time, she ushered Prudence gently out of her thoughts and was rewarded with a curt but respectful nod.

Delores turned her attention back to Gabriel. 'Don't worry about it,' she said. 'How're you feeling?'

'Like I've been hit by an avalanche.' He shivered and Delores reached for a blanket from the floor next to his bed.

Dr Reid stopped her. 'It doesn't help, and he finds the extra weight painful. Time and some quite specific apothecary will do the trick.' She picked up a small bottle made of deep-blue glass. It was fat and round at the bottom and topped with an ornate silver stopper. 'Tincture of Crimson Underwing: excellent for this particular malady.'

Gabriel shuddered. 'Please take me with you.' He laughed as he said it, but it still came out more of a plea than a joke.

Prudence buttoned the vintage tweed coat she was wearing; tightly fitted at the waist and flared towards her ankles, it echoed Ernaline Reid's distinctive style. Delores rolled her eyes.

Prudence caught it and glared at her. 'The Uncles want us downstairs. It's time to go.'

Delores leaned over and hugged Gabriel as gently as she could.

'I won't break,' he whispered.

Delores lingered, reluctant to let the moment pass. 'You'd better not.'

Prudence coughed to get Delores moving then swooped in to give Gabriel a quick peck on the forehead. As she did, Maud threw her arms around Prudence's neck, and the usually ice-cold illusionist barely stifled a sob. Maud held one hand out towards Delores and drew her into a group hug. Hesitant at first, Delores let herself relax into it, let the feeling of belonging wash over her.

Prudence bristled inside the embrace and when she could take the affection no longer, she broke away. 'We really have to go,' she whispered. 'The Uncles are getting restless.'

Delores gave Maud and Gabriel one last gentle squeeze and followed Prudence down the stairs towards their next adventure, together.

Whether they liked it or not.

ACKNOWLEDGEMENTS:

Thank you to everyone who has supported me on my creative adventures but especially...

Penny Thomas, Amy Low and everyone at Firefly for giving Delores a chance. Nathan Collins for seeing Delores so clearly, and Rosie Talbot and Leonie Lock for the fabulous cover reveal.

Matilda Johnson and Imogen Cooper at GEA for making it feel possible.

Sara Grant, the Undiscovered Voices team, and fellow UV2020s, Annaliese Avery, Anna Brooke, Adam Connors, Michael Mann, Helen MacKenzie, Sharon Boyle, Urara Hiroeh, Angela Murray, Clare Harlow, Harriet Worrell and Laura Warminger with special guests Chrissie Sains and Pascal Chind. Thank you for the beta reads, the pizzas, the translations and the friendship.

SCBWI Scotland's Linda MacMillan and The MG Critters, Onie Tibbitt and The Huddlers, cheerleader extraordinaire Sarah Broadley, and the lovely Justin Davies and Elizabeth Frattaroli.

Alice Broadway, Delores' first reader. I still have your gorgeous notes. Penelope Beck and Pete Thurlow for the bookish chat, Creative Scotland and The Scottish Book Trust for your support.

Cathy Johnson, thank you for your endless friendship and for listening to all my nonsense.

Lesley Scriven, you truly are Delores' Fairy Godmother.

And the Banhams, the Joneses and the Thurlow-Hogarth Collective for not minding my weird all that much. Carol, Tony and Kristina, and to my Mum who we all miss every day. Hope and Alexandra, for everything you've either knowingly or unwittingly contributed to this book. You breathed life into Delores and Prudence, put words in their mouths and clothes on their backs. But most of all Terry, who still doesn't believe in ghosts but has always believed in me.